THE CAPTAIN:

Colombian Waters

By Cam Séamus

The Captain: Colombian Waters

Cutwater Publishing

First Edition: 2024

ISBN: 978-1-7362349-5-2

Library of Congress Catalog Number 2024917919

Senior Editor - Laurie Taylor
Developmental Editor – Theodore Niekras
Editor – Kimberly Albury
Cover Design – The Book Designers

Learn more about the author: https://camseamus.com

Also by Cam Séamus

Fiction:
The Captain: Point Loma

Memoir:
Two Years Behind the Helm

For Laury,
The writer who kept me writing.

And cheerfully at Sea,
Success you still entice,
To get the pearl and gold…

-Michael Drayton
To the Virginia Voyage
1606

THE CAPTAIN:

Colombian Waters

1

The boat rolled hard. The captain was jolted awake as he slammed against the ceiling of his berth. Fighting through the fog of sleep, his mind tried to process what was happening. They were upside down in the water, hundreds of miles off the east coast of the United States. The Nor'easter pushing south against the Gulfstream had created teeth, and those teeth had just bitten the sailing yacht *Windborne*. "Brace," he tried to shout, but the words wouldn't form as he looked at Jen Campbell, lying next to him. Her pale, dead face was staring back at him as if frozen in time. Perplexed, he wondered, *How could she be dead?* He started to scream but nothing came out. Suddenly, it felt like the boat was spinning in a whirlpool and going down. He tried to move but felt paralyzed.

"Jennnnn!" He screamed in a muffled voice that sounded like something was over his face.

With great effort, Jack Kelly forced himself awake from the nightmare and slowly sat up in his berth – the last place where he had seen her alive.

"Forgive me, Jen. I'm so sorry, I'm so sorry." He got up and went into the boat's saloon.

The inside of *Windborne* had been put back together after the accident. All the books were in order from tallest to smallest. A hand-crafted teak rack that held the yacht's finest glassware hung next to a picture of Jack and Jen walking arm in arm on a white sandy beach. The navigation station was organized with charts and electronic equipment. On the main aft bulkhead of the saloon there was a large, framed photo of *Windborne* in her slip at Key West, with the U.S. yacht ensign standing tall in the gulf breezes. The inside of the boat appeared as if nothing had happened, but *everything* had happened. Despite the order that was present inside the boat, the outside was in a state of disarray, damage, and dysfunction. The state of the boat was the opposite of Jack - he was broken on the inside.

He looked around his home, which had also been her home. The intricate details inside the saloon were covered with Jen's fingerprints. She had transformed the yacht into something beautiful with throw pillows and nautical décor, along with an eye for the details that made the difference. It was one of the million things that he missed about her. Jack knew he could never leave *Windborne*, even though the boat came with all her memories.

The Coast Guard inquiry held at Portsmouth, Virginia had found Captain Jack Kelly guilty of dereliction of duty and stripped him of his captain's license for one year. It had been only a week since the trial, yet it felt much longer with each day bringing a renewed sense of despair.

Jack sat in *Windborne's* saloon, trying to resist the urge to open a new bottle of rum. It was a battle he knew he would eventually lose. The remedy to forget was simple – rum, as much as possible every day. But along the way, somewhere deep inside of him, he heard Jen's voice saying, *"Enough. You've got to move on."* He began tapering off the booze, but the urge to drink was as constant as the desire to forget.

Like a twisted mantra, he was repeating the same things in his mind. *How did I let this happen? How can I ever forgive myself? Will you ever forgive me?* On it went, every night and day since the accident. He knew he needed a distraction, so he grabbed his shower bag and headed up the gangway to the marina showers. Empty time had become his enemy, and the showers had become one of the many small rituals barely holding his fragile world together.

As he walked along the water to the shower, the realization that he needed a plan was thundering in his mind because money was drying up. Since he wasn't going to be able to work as a charter captain for a year, he needed a way to earn a living and re-fit the boat. The once proud captain had met the demons that had brought him to his knees: loss, failure, and self-despair. As Jack wrestled with them, he was losing ground.

The marina showers had been washing the salt and sweat off boaters since the 1970's with few improvements since they had been built. The old, off-white tiled stalls were kept reasonably clean, and occasionally, the plywood dividers were treated to a fresh coat of epoxy paint with leftovers from the yard. This was a marina built for the working class. It waited patiently, without pretense, for boats and boat owners that had seen better days. There were no yachts or clubs. It had a run-down office occupied by a woman who chain-smoked while trying to collect on the many past due accounts, along with a small work yard, a reliable deli, and a dingy bar. It was a place where no one asked you what came before. It suited Jack perfectly.

A dank smell with a hint of bleach hit Jack's nostrils as he walked into the bathroom. Glancing at himself in the mirror as he slipped out of his clothes, he thought he looked older and tired. Stepping into the shower and turning the mixer to a cool setting on this very humid night, he buried his head in the spray, tried to relax, and began thinking about his options.

"*Day work*?" he said to himself, recalling his days in Fort Lauderdale where he began his career working on yachts. Jack didn't really want to go anywhere that he and Jen had been together, but he knew it was his best option. He could make money fast and his network was already established. *No, there's got to be something else*, he thought. The fear of reliving a happy past in a pain-filled present forced him to consider alternatives.

After finishing the shower, he began drying himself with a towel in front of the mirror and noticed the cuts in his abdominal muscles that were not the result of an exercise routine. The already lean man had dropped twenty pounds since the accident. The mirror revealed a thin waist that angled out to broad shoulders which still held some of the tan developed during the charter season. Alone in the bathroom, he looked at the fading tan and wondered if he too could just fade out. *Is there anywhere I can just run to and leave this all behind*?" He opened his shaving kit, took out the bar of shaving soap, and began to lather up his face. *I can't run with Windborne in her condition.* The man was also smart enough to realize that the problems and memories could run just as fast and far as he could. Nevertheless, he indulged the fantasies.

The dismasted sailboat would need a partial refit with a new mast, sails, boom, stanchions, and lifelines, not to mention an update to her electronics. Jack estimated that it would be seventy-five to a hundred thousand dollars. The insurance would take care of a good portion, but he would need cash. Cash to fix things, pay boatyard charges, and buy his meals. He'd worked on boats long enough to know that a boatyard could empty a wallet faster than a roulette table in Vegas. He realized that it might take him a year to earn enough money if he worked every waking minute and spent next to nothing on himself.

Jack leaned in towards the mirror drawing the razor across his cheek, thinking momentarily how easy it would be to remove the steel blade and slit his wrists. As if his thought had tempted fate, the blade took a taste of him. "Damnit!" he said as the blood rolled down his cheek. He held a tissue on the cut and reminded himself, *Don't lose focus, Jack. Bad shit happens when you lose focus.*

He looked at his hair and noticed how long and shaggy it had gotten over the last few months.

"Maybe a beach crew cut this time?"

Jack was talking to himself a lot because he hadn't yet acclimated to being alone. It was part of the transition of a life that had gone from carefree to chaos. The once proud and carefree captain felt powerless and hopeless.

He zipped up the shaving kit and wrapped a beach towel around his waist before making the short walk back to the boat in the warm evening air. As he walked along the waterfront toward his dock gate, he looked up through the bar window and noticed a fishing boat on the TV. Then he saw the title *Alaskan Captains* flash across the screen.

"Alaska, maybe that's where I need to go."

Jack felt a momentary surge of hope that there might be a place other than Fort Lauderdale – somewhere without all of the reminders. But he also knew that a greenhorn on a fishing boat wouldn't get a good share of the money, and once again, he'd be at the bottom of the industry. He began to think about it more practically, *Lauderdale has a massive marine industry – parts, skilled labor, good yards, yeah, that's the place we need to be.* He was determined to bring *Windborne* back to her former glory, if not for himself, at least to honor the memory of Jen.

The former captain's resolve began building with a glimmer of hope as he thought, *Tomorrow will be the start of a new chapter for me and Windborne. We'll prepare to make our way down the Atlantic Intracoastal Waterway.* A smirk of sarcasm formed on his lips as he thought about the once beautiful sailing yacht on the inland waterway. *It's the perfect route to Fort Lauderdale for a non-sailing sailboat.*

Jack also knew what he would do for the rest of the night. One at a time, he would carefully take out the pictures of Jen, and keep drinking rum until he could no longer see her face.

2

Jack sat on the beach and gazed at the massive twenty-mile bridge-tunnel crossing the Chesapeake. The overcast day suited his mood perfectly. Pairs of old pier pilings made their way into the water from the shore, like a path to the past which evoked memories of what had once been. The nostalgia attached itself to his restless soul like a barnacle on one of the pilings. The energy of his plan from the night before had faded with the rum. He sat and brooded.

He thought about what he considered his sins and how to unburden himself, *Bury the sins deeply, and with them, her memory.* However, Jack's problem was that he wanted to remember and forget at the same time. He longed to hear her softly call his name and feel her gentle caress. He desperately wanted to hold her. He was learning that it was impossible to experience the past or the present when you were stuck in one or the other. Jack was trapped between two realities.

Despite his efforts to remember only the good memories, he could hear her scream the last words he heard her say, "He's gone Jack, he's gone." It played in his mind like a tape recorder in an endless loop. Then he would think about Dave, the charter guest that had died in the accident. The trip down memory lane wouldn't be complete without remembering the night he slept with Dave's girlfriend Mallory - more guilt. Jack was crawling deeper and deeper into a very dark hole, having no idea of how dangerous it is to live in the dark.

Lost deep in his own mind, he heard her scream again, but something was different this time, it wasn't Jen's voice. Something didn't add up, and he began to retrace his steps out of the dark hole. Then, he heard it again, but more clearly this time.

"Help! Somebody, please help!"

Jack looked over toward the direction of the sound and saw a woman chest deep in the water. She was screaming for help and waving her arms above her head. Instinctively, he was on his feet and running toward her.

She screamed again, "Oh my God, No! Help, please!"

Jack was now in a full sprint across the beach. He could see that the woman was standing in the water and not in any danger, so he began scanning out further, where he found the cause of her fear and urgency. A young girl was on a body board a little over a hundred feet from the beach and a large dorsal fin was cutting the water around her. As Jack got closer, he heard her tiny voice pleading for help through sobs.

"Help me, momma. Please!"

The shark had taken an interest in the little girl, making continual circles and coming closer with each one. Jack knew he didn't have much time to get to her and barely stopped at the water's edge to drop his pants and tear off his shirt before plunging into the ocean.

He could still hear the mother screaming uncontrollably, but now it seemed distant because Jack was laser focused on the shark and the girl. His mind shut out everything else as he felt his heart pounding in his chest. He bounded into the water as he had been taught during a Jr. Lifeguard course – always keeping his eyes on the girl. Just as it became deep enough to start swimming, he saw the shark bump the board, which flipped the little girl into the water. He knew that the shark was probably just curious, but sometimes they explore things with an unintentionally deadly bite.

Now stroking hard toward the girl with his head-up and out of the water, he kept his eyes darting between her and the shark. His lungs felt like they were going to burst as he pulled hard and kicked with fierce determination. To Jack's relief, the shark had taken a wide loop that bought him the time he needed. Just as he reached her, he saw the shark turn and head directly toward them. Jack placed himself between the girl and the shark and began treading water as he grabbed the body board.

Then he said to her, "You're gonna swim, okay?"

"Yeah," she replied through her tears.

"Get to shore as fast as you can! Go!"

The shark accelerated towards Jack and the thought of death flashed through his mind, *Maybe the ocean has decided to finish me off.* Swimming sidestroke so he could maintain a visual on the predator, he placed the thin foam body board between himself and its razor-sharp teeth and took a few quick strokes. When he realized it was shallow enough to stand, he walked backwards as fast as possible, keeping his eyes locked on the shark. As Jack stood chest deep in the water, the ancient killing machine came right at him. A quick glance back at the girl reassured him that she was safe because he could see her mother pulling her out of the water. Jack turned his attention back to the shark right before it hit. The board was ripped out of his hands with unimaginable force as he came face to face with a mouth full of terrifying teeth. The Chondrichthyes fish thrashed violently as it tore into the bodyboard and ripped it apart.

Seizing the moment when the shark's attention was on the board, he turned and swam hard until he reached thigh deep water. Just as he stood up, he felt the shark bump against his leg, and he watched the dorsal fin cutting the water as it began a circle that would end up right where he stood. With adrenaline pumping through his body, Jack moved with incredible speed and agility as he ran through the shallow water with his feet clearing the surface each time he took a stride. Finally, reaching the beach beyond the water's edge, he collapsed in exhaustion as the young Great White shark swam back out into the deep.

"Holy crap," was all that Jack could manage to say, nearly breathless from the exertion.

A voice from behind caught his attention as the mother approached, "Oh my God, thank you! You saved Jenny's life. God bless you. God bless you," she said as she knelt and threw her arms around him.

"Jenny, did you say her name was Jenny?"

"Yes, my sweet girl, you saved her, oh my God. I never learned to swim – my father is a Coast Guard officer and I never learned to swim! Thank you, thank you."

They held onto each other for moments that felt like minutes, until Jack solemnly said, "I know that feeling of helplessness. Nothing feels worse."

The mother nervously laughed as she stood up and offered Jack a hand. She could see that he was still regaining his breath and composure, shaking, and panting as his body began to reset itself and clear the adrenaline that had probably saved their lives.

Jenny sheepishly approached him and through teary eyes, she said, "Tha-tha, thank you."

She looked up deeply into his eyes as tears rolled down her soft cheeks.

At the sound of her innocent voice and the knowledge of her name, Jack dropped to his knees, hugged her tightly, and started sobbing along with her.

"Oh, you poor thing, bless you!" the woman said as she knelt down and put her arms around both of them, "you must have been terrified too."

She joined in their tears.

"It's not that. It's just..." he trailed off and started sobbing again, "It's just that I recently lost someone at sea and her name was Jen."

"Oh, you poor dear, I'm so sorry!"

She continued to hold onto Jack as he slowly regained his composure and stood back up. He hadn't felt a woman's touch for some time and had nearly forgotten how comforting it was.

The little girl went about dutifully collecting Jack's clothing and flip-flops strewn along the beach and sweetly handed the bundle to him without a word. He began toweling himself off a little with his t-shirt when he suddenly became aware he was in his underwear. He doubled down on the dressing speed, pulling his shirt over his head, and quickly slipping on his pants. Finally, he brushed some sand off himself and said, "My name is Jack Kelly."

"Well, it's certainly a miracle to know you, Jack Kelly. I'm Laura. Do you live here?"

"I'm here with my boat," he said as he motioned towards the direction of the marina on the other side of the bridge. "We were in an accident in June, and I ended up here."

Laura followed the progression in the sentence from 'we' to 'I' and realized that the loss of *his* Jen might be the difference in that equation.

"Well, my dad is a senior officer at the Coast Guard base if you need anything, I'll put in a word for you," she said and then smiled and flashed her eyes at him.

It was the first time he noticed how beautiful she was as her chestnut, shoulder length hair sparkled in the emerging sunshine. She had a few freckles, soft features, and gentle curves.

"That is an offer I could have taken advantage of last month when they pulled my license for a year."

"I'm sorry to hear that. My dad is one of the officers that adjudicates those types of hearings."

After a little more back and forth, they realized that Laura's father had been the one who had harshly admonished Jack and stripped him of his master's credential.

"Small world," Jack chuckled at the irony.

"I do believe that everything happens for a reason. Like if you hadn't been here, my Jen might be dead right now."

Jack thought about what she said for a moment before saying, "I wish I could believe that somehow there is a purpose… that we're all connected, but I just can't get there."

"I understand, and you've been through a lot," she said with a smile that belayed understanding and compassion.

"Here's what we are going to do," she said. "You are going to go back to the boat and get cleaned up, and I am going to fix you a home cooked meal."

"I probably shouldn't... It's just-"

"Nonsense!" she interrupted him, "I will not take no for an answer."

Jack smiled and said, "All right then, dinner it is. Can I bring something?"

"No, don't you worry yourself one bit about anything, you just show up."

Laura took out a pen and notebook from her purse, writing down her phone number and address.

"Is seven o'clock okay?" She said as she handed him the paper.

"Yeah, sounds good."

Both of them had been so focused on the events that they hadn't noticed the crowd of onlookers that had gathered around them. People were filming with their phones, and some approached to offer their appreciation for Jack Kelly's heroism.

Jack didn't think it was heroism, he hadn't really *thought* at all. It was the response of a man who knew better than to ever go off duty again. By the time they sat down for dinner that evening, the former captain's exploits would be headlining the evening news.

3

Jack arrived at Laura's a few minutes early. He thanked the driver and slid out of the car with a small plastic bag in hand. The house was a traditional white colonial style, with the trim painted in a rich navy blue. Four large columns supported a massive porch balcony, and rich mahogany shutters graced hand crafted casement windows. An old, brick walkway lined with columns invited visitors to the beautiful home.

As he approached the house, he felt awkward and nervous, like he was on a first date. He reminded himself that it was not a date. Although, he had gone to some lengths to look presentable by borrowing an iron from the canvas repair lady and ironing his khakis, digging out a new company polo shirt embroidered with *Windborne Escapes,* and ditching the flip flops for a dressy pair of boat shoes. Jack had even managed to squeeze in a buzz cut at the old barber shop in town. He had cleaned up well.

After straightening his shirt, he walked up the path to the house and rang the doorbell. Dogs unleashed a sudden alarm, and he saw Jenny peer through the glass on the side of the front door and exclaim loud enough to be heard outside,

"Mommy, he's here! He's here!" A few seconds later, the door opened to Laura's smiling face, with Jenny at her side.

"Jack!" Laura said with enthusiasm, "I'm so happy you made it."

Jack smiled.

"I don't recall having much choice in the matter."

"Yeah, I guess you didn't. Com'on in," she said in a slightly southern accent as she opened the door wider and stepped to the side.

She was a few inches shorter than Jack, which he hadn't noticed at the beach. Her hair was pulled back into a ponytail, and she wore no makeup aside from some lip gloss. The jeans were tight and flattered her shape, while her blouse gathered in at the waist, with a few buttons open at the top. Jack guessed her age at about thirty-five and he found her incredibly attractive.

"Jack, Jack," Jenny screamed as she threw her arms around him.

Jack patted her on the head and said, "Hey, kiddo! I brought you something." He reached into the bag and pulled out a small plastic shark. "I don't want you to be scared of these guys – odds are that you'll never see one again. But you can play with this one and make sure he knows who's boss!"

"Thank you, Jack!" she said as she ran off to play with the shark on the couch.

The resiliency of children amazed him. He was envious.

Jack looked down and noticed that the two pointers were standing patiently and wagging their tails. He waved them over saying, "Here." The dogs gleefully obeyed, their tails now wagging so hard that their back ends were shifting from side to side as he patted them on the head and scratched their backs.

"I always scratch the backs of dogs," he said with a warm smile. "And dogs seem to remember who scratches their back."

Laura smiled at the comment.

"Jack, I hope you like southern fried chicken, mashed potatoes, and sweet peas. I didn't think to ask you. Then, I'm at the store trying to figure it out," she pauses and glances playfully at Jenny, "and *someone* keeps chirping in my ear about baking you a cake. I went into autopilot, grabbed a chicken and some russets. The peas are from our own garden, and Jenny picked them herself!"

From the couch, Jenny paused her play and hopefully smiled up at Jack for approval.

"I love peas young lady – thank you for picking them."

"What about the cake?" Jack quipped.

"Oh, yes, and the cake is vanilla with chocolate icing – Jenny thought you would like that. She seemed quite sure of it. But I suspect that it may be 'cause it's *her* favorite. Isn't that right, Jenny?"

Jenny smiled again, looking to Jack for approval.

"I do love that," he lied effortlessly and winked at Laura.

"Jenny, you go finish gathering up the horses in your room. I'll call you for dinner in a few minutes." Then, turning to Jack she said, "She loves those stuffed horses."

Jack looked around and said, "Your home is beautiful, Laura."

"It's a bit traditional for my taste, it belonged to my father and mother. After mom passed, and Dan passed – he was my husband – my father decided to move back to base. He gave the house to me and Jenny."

"Sounds like an amazing man. I wish I'd had a better chance to get to know him, but under the circumstances…" He smiled at her halfheartedly and cocked his head.

"Well, you will. Don't be mad, but when he heard what happened, he insisted on joining us for dinner."

"Wow. Sure, that's great," Jack said in his best attempt at authenticity. The thought of the officer's presence at dinner made him very uncomfortable.

"He wanted to thank you in person, and who knows, maybe it'll be considered when they re-evaluate your license."

"Yeah, maybe. I need all the help I can get."

"Let me show you around."

Laura gave him a quick tour of the house. Jack noticed the pictures of her husband, who had been a decorated Navy SEAL. There was a folded,

American flag in a wood and glass frame that hung on the wall, with a SEAL trident on the frame. Then he saw the framed Medal of Honor, along with rows of ribbons and medals beneath the flag.

"May I ask what happened?"

"He was killed during an operation. Before he died, he dragged out three of his team members to safety. I try to picture him saving his friends, then I see him bleeding and dying. Over and over again. I swear to you, I cannot get those images out of my mind. Images my imagination created of things I could never see… of things I should never have had to see."

"God, I'm so sorry. I shouldn't have asked."

"No, it's alright, I don't get to talk about it much. Given that you lost someone, I figure you can understand what I'm going through."

"Yeah, I do." said Jack. "Do you have nightmares?"

Laura nodded and wiped her right eye. Jack instinctively reached for her and put his arms around her. His intimacy with pain gave him the knowledge that it often retreated in the face of kindness and compassion.

"Thank you," she said as he pulled away.

"No worries," said Jack.

Jack's phone and the doorbell rang almost simultaneously, sending the dogs into full alert mode as the barking echoed off the hardwood floors.

"That's probably my dad at the door," she said.

Jack replied, “Do you mind if I take this call?” as the phone continued to ring.

“Perfectly fine. It’ll be a few more minutes before dinner is ready. You can use the study.” She motioned to a room on the right that they hadn’t toured yet.

“Thanks,” said Jack.

He walked into the study and answered his phone.

“This is Jack.”

“Jack, you dirty pirate son of a bitch, it’s Pablo!”

“Pablo, you captain of pirates! How the heck are ya?”

Jack and Pablo had become friends when Jack worked in the super-yacht industry, and he had twice chartered the yacht on which Jack crewed. After the other guests had retired to their staterooms, Pablo would often have a nightcap while Jack was on watch. They would talk about sailboats, islands, palm trees, and pirates. Jack felt like he was the most down-to-earth multi-millionaire that he’d ever met, although it seemed peculiar that Pablo wanted to spend time alone with him at night. He also sensed that Pablo was hiding something behind all of that money. Despite his questions about Pablo or his motives, Jack felt inexplicably drawn to him, and worked extra hard to ensure that he had a good cruise – which Pablo rewarded abundantly.

“I’m good, I’m good, Jack. I need a lift though.”

Unconsciously forgetting about his license and the state of his boat, Jack asked, "From where to where?"

"Fort Lauderdale to Colombia, round trip."

Jack paused and let that sink in.

"Jack? Did I lose you?"

"No, I'm still here," Jack said after the long pause. He was trying to buy time to think because nothing about that statement sounded right. *Who sails from Florida to Colombia round trip on a sailboat unless it's part of a cruising circuit?*

Jack suddenly recalled the feeling he'd had when he agreed to that fateful charter. This felt the same way. Yet, there was another part of Jack emerging from underneath - an underlying dark current was washing over him. Despite his sudden disregard for the law, he knew the smart money would be to pass on Pablo's offer graciously and without pissing him off. Jack estimated that he could be either a good friend, or a terrifying enemy.

"Ah, thanks for thinking of me Pablo, but I lost my license, and my boat needs a full refit. We got rolled by a rogue wave in a storm. I've got to earn some dough to get it all done. It'll probably be a year before she's ready for sea, and I don't even know if they will reinstate me or not."

The line was silent for a moment, then Pablo spoke.

"How long would it take if you had the money?"

"Maybe a month – if I could find a yard that has capacity."

"¿Cuanto dinero?"

"Anyone's guess, probably at least a hundred thou less what the insurance will cover."

"So, what if I paid the yard, and paid you another twenty for the ride?"

"Pablo, I..." He suddenly realized he might be having a criminal conversation a few feet away from the man that would ultimately decide his fate as a captain.

"Pablo, I'm not in a good place to talk now. Can I call you in the morning?"

"Of course, my friend, of course. Call this number that I called you from."

Jack looked at the caller ID.

"Got it, talk to you tomorrow, Pablo."

Pablo said goodbye and Jack hung up the phone just as Laura poked her head in the door.

"Dinner's ready, Jack."

"Great, I'm starving."

They walked out of the study and down the hall lined with her husband's photos and awards. Jack felt a twinge of failure and guilt as he walked past the brave man's memorial. They passed under an archway and into a formal dining room, where Laura's father and Jenny were already seated at the table.

The look on the Commander's face was warmer and friendlier than the last time the two men had met. The officer looked intently into his eyes and said, "Jack Kelly, I may owe you an apology."

4

Dinner had been pleasant, and Laura's father was very reassuring that Jack would be reinstated at the one-year mark, if not sooner. For some reason, that assurance made him more uncomfortable. He was glad to have a high-ranking friend in the Coast Guard – it could come in handy someday. Her father had all but said outright that Jack had a marker, and he could call it in when needed.

Back on *Windborne*, Jack began the process of prepping for the short trip down the waterway. There were plenty of places to stop along the way, but he preferred to have certain items in stock on the boat, so he took his inventory. It was also reminiscent of how he and Jen had operated the charter. The damaged man clung to his routines. When he finished, he sat down with a hot cup of coffee and called Pablo.

"Pablo, it's Jack."

"Captain Jack! I'm so glad you called, my friend. We have many plans to discuss, you and I, yes?"

"Perhaps, but I have some questions."

"Ask away, my friend."

"Does this involve running drugs?"

Pablo let out a hearty laugh.

"I think you misunderstand my purpose here. I need a long break, and I want to see my family in Colombia – that's all."

"Okay, I get that. But why are you trying to hire a guy with a screwed-up boat – you could hire any guy you want."

"I don't want to be at sea with someone I don't like – this is a lesson you once shared with me, Jack. I believe you said, 'Make sure they're not assholes before you leave the dock, because once you're out there, you can't just toss them off the boat.'" Pablo paused before continuing. "We've been on the water together, and I definitely like you. You know what you're doing, and you have a good sense of humor."

"One could argue that if I knew what I was doing, my boat would still have a mast instead of a stump."

Pablo laughed at the joke.

"See, this is what I mean. Plus, I get to help you out. I've got plenty of cash, my friend. I need places to spend it."

"That sounds like a nice problem, Pablo."

Jack thought for a moment. The dark part of him that was rising from below shouted, *carpe diem,* while his morals screamed, *run!* Ultimately, the darker voice wormed its way to the forefront.

"Well, I'm up in Virginia, it's a good hopping off point for the route I'd take to Colombia. I could get the work done up here and you could fly up when it's time to leave. How's that sound?"

There was a long silence as Jack waited nervously. Suddenly, he saw Pablo as a source of instant salvation. *I can get Windborne back to sea and away from this damned marina.* Jack desperately wanted to be away from land and its inhabitants, who reminded him of nothing more than failure and death. He didn't know if the open ocean was the answer, but he had to find out if there would be any peace for him once he reached the bluewater depths.

Finally, Pablo answered him, "I know some people down here Jack; some owe me. I think it would be better if you brought the boat down here."

"I was thinking about heading to Fort Lauderdale anyway, but that would add sea time to the Colombia trip. Are you good with that?"

"Yes, that's fine, Jack. I want a long trip – hell, I need a long trip. But I don't understand how going further south adds time?"

"It's a sailboat my friend, the route to Colombia takes us up and around the Bahamas. If you try to head due south, it's not favorable from a wind and current standpoint. People do it, but..."

"I have much to learn from you! Perhaps you will even teach me to sail – it's time for a new hobby. Ok, that settles it, you will come down here."

It wasn't a question.

"I have a guy in Fort Lauderdale who owns a yard. It's better to be down here, around people I know and *trust*... Yes?" Pablo emphasized the word trust.

Jack hesitated for a moment; his moral indicators were bouncing around. However, he also felt a sudden sense of relief that someone else was in charge. Under Pablo's care, he might shake off this interminable sense of responsibility.

"Cool. Pablo, I can't thank you enough. I've been sitting around thinking about how to put it all back together."

"No thanks are necessary my friend. Sometimes things happen for a reason."

There it was again, the idea that it's all by design. *Who knows…* Jack wondered.

"Roger that, Pablo. Well, it's about a thousand nautical miles to Lauderdale and for the most part I'm going to travel during the day, so we're looking at a couple of weeks. I'll ring you when I'm close and we can connect on the rest of the details. Text me the name and location of the yard." Jack paused, and then asked with humility, "You sure you want to hang your hat with a defrocked captain?"

Without hesitation he answered, "I'm sure, my friend, perhaps we will become pirates together."

After their goodbyes, Jack hung up the phone and said to himself, "*Pirates?* Yeah, maybe we'll do just that..."

Jack was sensing an emerging recklessness in his attitude. He was certain that Pablo wasn't telling him everything. *Who cares? What does any of it matter? None of it brings her back.*

He continued his preparations and began to think out loud.

“Provision list ready. Charts are organized and in order. Float plan to leave with… Laura – she'll take it. Deckhand, I want to find a deckhand.”

He jotted down a few more notes and then carefully double checked his list. He would forever be more cautious than he had been in the past. After he completed his list, he opened his computer and logged onto the marina Wi-Fi. In his browser, he pulled up his favorites, clicked on a crew sharing website and posted a message.

Vessel: Windborne. Job: Two weeks paid boat move southbound on the AICW. Pay: $100 per day, provisions, and flight paid round trip. Expected: Good attitude, clean, non-smoker, standard watchkeeping duties and chores. Timing: Need to leave asap, trip will take about two weeks. Contact: Message me on this board.

With the preparations in order, Jack headed out to do some shopping for the trip. He realized that this was the first time he'd provisioned since Key West. That realization came with an eerie feeling that washed over his soul. In some ways, he felt like he was embarking on another doomed trip. In other ways, he felt like he was starting a new life and career. Endless pushing and pulling between these perceived realities would continue to dominate his waking hours; the nightmares would dominate the rest.

5

Pablo sat at the streetside café in the Little Havana neighborhood in Miami. He was sipping a Café Cubano, and letting the sweet sugary foam linger in his mouth a few seconds before swallowing. He took in the bright colors of the neighborhood and closed his eyes as he breathed in the mixture of aromas from flowers, bakeries, and of course, the coffee. He removed the dark black sunglasses and Panama hat, running his fingers through his thick, wavy black hair. He was stylishly dressed in linen pants, a Havana style shirt, and woven leather shoes. The man's skin was a rich, light brown. A broad nose with a bulbous tip stood watch over a ruddy face. While he stood at only 5'8" tall, he seemed like a much bigger man, in part due to his charisma and presence, and in part due to the general thickness of his frame.

Looking at his watch, he saw that it was time to make the call. He pulled a burner phone out of his pocket and dialed a number scrawled on a small notebook page.

"Hola, Don Julio, this is Pablo."

"Hola, mi amigo. ¿Como estás?"

"I am well, Jefe. How are the grandchildren?"

"They are smiling and happy, as all children should be. Speaking of family, is there a woman for you yet?"

"No. I'm busy with work, which is why I'm calling. I've arranged my transportation," he paused mid-sentence, looking around to ensure that no one was within earshot before he continued, "and I think it's safe to say that we will not arouse any suspicion."

"¿Por qué?"

"I've decided that I'm in need of a long sail, on a cruising sailboat. There are thousands of them - they come and go largely unnoticed."

"Bueno," said the Don. "Have you corrected the problem in Miami?"

"Sí, that is no longer a concern," said Pablo.

Don Julio inquired further, "I would like to see evidence."

"We saved his famous gold tooth with the mark; I will bring it with me to Colombia."

"You always know the right way to do these unpleasant things, my son."

"Thank you, Papa." Pablo rarely referred to his father in such an endearing way, their relationship was professional, and at times volatile and violent. It was never completely honest.

"See you in a few months, Jefe," said Pablo.

"Goodbye, Pablo."

He drained the last drops of the syrupy espresso and smiled with satisfaction, knowing that he had pleased his father.

6

At his home, Pablo lay in his bed listening to the sound of the running fountain. He could hear the birds chirping as they jockeyed for position around the feeder. He gazed out the window at the bright red mandevilla vine and then closed his eyes as his mind drifted back to the birds on his family's rancho in Colombia.

As if through someone else's eyes, he watched a dove feeding, and then suddenly saw its chest explode in a ball of feathers. A shotgun blast had transformed it from life to death. He could feel a tear coming in his eye but knew that his father would see this as a sign of weakness; that would mean another beating. He quickly wiped his eye, then looked down at the gun in his hands, *Why am I holding the gun? Why did I shoot the bird? It was innocent. What have I done?*

Pablo woke up suddenly, as if startled, and realized that he had drifted off for a few minutes. He sat up in bed and felt that his eyes were indeed moist, and he wiped them deliberately. The old memory had done its work, and he was soon on a journey retracing the path of proving absolute love and loyalty to his father, Don Julio. Shooting the bird was only the beginning.

The Don's family listened intently as young Pablo proudly recounted the fight at the dinner table.

"I stood my ground, Papa. The way that you taught me to."

"Who won?" asked the big man.

"I think it was even, Papa."

"There's no such thing as even. It's always win or lose. Remember that!" He slammed his fist on the table. The man had not yet become a Don, he was a high-ranking lieutenant for the local cartel. People had learned to fear him, especially his own family.

"Come here boy."

Pablo nervously got up from his seat and walked over to the big man. The Don straightened the boy out by grabbing his shoulders forcefully.

"Is there any such thing as even?"

"No Papa, win or lose only."

His father drew back his closed fist and hit the boy across the side of his mouth and face, knocking him to the floor and nearly unconscious. His mother and aunt shrieked but said nothing. They knew better. Both leaped to their feet to attend to the boy.

"Leave him! He needs to stand on his own!"

His father returned to his meal, while Pablo fought to get up. It took him over a minute to get back on his feet and dry his tears. Tears his father permitted, only because he had hit him so hard. The big man looked the boy in the eye.

"Did you win or lose that round?"

"I lost, Papa," he snuffled.

"Beat this boy at school and bring me proof, or I will hit you even harder tomorrow night."

Young Pablo had done as commanded. He found the boy before school and beat him so severely that an ambulance was called. While the boy lay on the gurney, Pablo walked over, grabbed the crucifix which hung around his neck and ripped it off him saying, "I guess your God isn't much for saving his own people in a fight, or maybe he just doesn't care about you, Cucaracha."

The other children laughed when Pablo called him cockroach, but after seeing what their classmate was capable of, they were terrified. From that day forward, they showed extreme deference to him. Pablo could feel a sense of control as they cleared out of his way. At this young age began the unquenchable drive for him to consolidate power.

Pablo learned that with power came permission. Because of his connection to the cartel, there was no disciplinary action taken against him at school because the school administrators knew who and what his father was. That night at the dinner, Pablo proudly walked up to his father who was seated at the end of the table and dropped the crucifix in front of him.

"The cockroach was stepped on, Papa."

His father picked up the crucifix and spun it gently in his hands, then he looked at his son and said, "And what of the boy?"

"He took a ride in the ambulance to the hospital."

His father wound up and hit him again, knocking him to the floor. This time, the boy who was learning to become a dangerous man did not cry. Instead, he picked himself up faster and stood in front of his father without fear.

"What was that for Papa?"

"That was to teach you what people can do to you if they want revenge. You left this boy alive. Who is to say that he won't come back and try to kill you or your family." He waved his big hand around the table at Pablo's mother, aunt, and sisters.

"Next time, do not be so generous. Next time, kill what needs to be killed."

"Yes, Papa. Kill what needs to be killed. I understand."

As he lay in bed, he thought, *Yes, Papa, kill what needs to be killed. I remember my first one – my 16th birthday when you let me earn our crest.* Sometimes he tried to remember, but mostly he tried to forget. The price had not been too high because it had purchased his father's respect, which he prized above all other things. He looked back out the window at the mandevilla vine and drifted off to an uneasy sleep.

7

The trip down the Intracoastal Waterway had gone smoother than expected. In Jack's imagination, there was another journey with storms and emergencies that ended with the boat sinking only feet from the shore. But none of that happened, it was a predictable, easy passage. *Windborne was* now three days from Fort Lauderdale and at the moment, passing through a narrow, tree-lined section of the canal. Jack was enjoying the warmth of the sun directly overhead and a few moments of peace. The man's normally turbulent mind was remarkably still.

The deckhand was proving herself to be a good fit and Jack was considering offering her a place on the Colombia trip. If she was interested, he would have to run it by Pablo. That was not standard for charter operations, but this was already anything but standard. Jack was settling into the new structure.

He looked forward where Mariana was inspecting lines for chafe.

"How do they look?" he called out.

"Not terrible, skipper. But I'd probably pull them and keep them as back-ups."

"Alright, add it to the list," said Jack.

"Running out of paper," she replied humorously.

"Yeah, it's gonna break the bank."

These were the moments of solace tucked neatly inside his moral and legal concerns about Pablo. Whenever he thought about the price tag, he knew Pablo wouldn't care. But he wondered how big that marker was going to be when Pablo finally called it in. *I can't think about that right now.*

"Mariana."

"Yeah, Cap."

"Sit down with me for a few minutes."

Jack kept a light hand on the helm as they floated down the canal.

"I've got a round trip to Colombia, and I need a first mate - you interested?"

"Same rate?"

"Yep."

"Sure, I'm interested."

"I've got a client that will need to approve you to join the group; if you can win him over, you've got the gig."

"Cool. Thanks, Cap."

Mariana stood up and Jack noticed her height again. *Must be 6'1" at least,* he thought as he watched her bump her head on the saloon-top as she went down. It happened with regularity, and her response was predictable. First, she'd let out a good-natured laugh, then run her hand through her shoulder length, thick, reddish-brown hair to straighten it. Finally, she would kiss her fingers and touch them on the ceiling.

"Why do you do that thing with kissing your fingers and touching the ceiling?" Jack called down to her.

"My mom said, 'find something good about the thing that just bothered you and give it a kiss.' I think about how glad I'll be to have this roof over my head when it rains, and I give it a kiss. She was teaching me to find good in things - to appreciate all that surrounds us."

"Wow, deep."

"She grew up very poor; for some people it might have left them bitter, but for mom, it left her grateful."

"Good perspective," Jack said as he nodded in agreement.

Jack had not wanted a woman on his crew because he didn't trust himself emotionally and he didn't want to get tangled up with someone. When he first met her, he thought she looked like a Viking princess. Her stature was as impressive as her understated beauty, and her personality was clearly a good match for his own. She was tough, yet gentle, and had a great sense of humor. After her interview, he lied and said he had a few more people to interview, hoping that he would find a man. But the applicant pool had been thin on such short notice, and the men that applied were duds. Mariana was talented, credentialed, and the best sailor for the job.

As she came back on deck, he studied her features and noticed her pronounced jaw and the small overbite. As she pulled the hair away from her face, he could get a better look at the tattoos on her neck. One side of her head was shaved, which Jack found very enticing for some reason. *Late twenties, a little young but…* Then thoughts of Jen invaded his imagination and Mariana was gone. Suddenly, he found himself in a room with Jen. There with no doors or windows and the light was fading fast. He reached out to touch Jen's face when five sharp blasts, along with Mariana's shouting, called him back.

"JACK! Alter course to starboard. NOW!" She screamed as she rushed back toward the helm that was in his hands.

As Mariana jerked the helm to the right, Jack looked up and saw the working dredge which had the right of way. She put her hands on his shoulders and looked him directly in the eyes.

"You ok, Cap? You looked as if you were not here. You should go down and rest a bit. I'll take the helm for a while and holler if I need you."

"I don't want you up here alone, something could happen."

"Sure, it could, Jack. And if it does, we'll sort it out."

"At least clip in, okay?" He asked in desperation rather than ordering her to do so.

"Jack, we're in a protected waterway and the weather is calm. I'm not feeling the need for a harness."

"What if you fall overboard?"

"Jesus, what happened to you out there?"

Jack said nothing, he just shook his head and turned to go below. He had only told her part of the story, being too embarrassed to talk about the deaths of Jen and Dave.

Mariana had spent enough time around people who lived and worked on the water; she'd seen a few that had been broken by the ocean and recognized some of it in Jack. *Broken is a dangerous quality in a captain.* She thought as she watched him go down below. *I'll keep a closer eye on him from now on.*

8

Pablo sat at a small Colombian café, with bandeja paisa set before him. The dish had been one of his father's favorites, and it was a pleasant childhood memory. He thought of his family at the dinner table, enjoying a good meal together. Most nights, his father would not flare up at dinner. The man thought of his father often, and in many ways, he was still a small boy trying to please him. *Oh Papa, you would love this café!* But travel to the US wasn't possible for his father, given that Don Julio was on the DEA's top ten wanted list.

Pablo considered the trip to Colombia and started making a list of what needed to be loaded onto the boat. He began to calculate the total area he would need to transport everything, and when he had finished, he called the boatyard.

"Juan, how are you, my friend."

"Buenas tardes, Señor Pablo. What can I do for you today?"

"Did you receive the information I sent over on the boat?"

"Yes, I have reviewed it."

"We will need compartments built, a total of two cubic feet for the heavy inventory, and some longer ones that could take tubes up to three feet in length and some irregularly shaped items. All of them will need to be out of the way and concealed to match the paint. Can you do this on this particular model of sailboat?"

"Jefe, you know I will always do what you ask. It will present challenges because sailboats do not have a lot of unused space. But we will find a way. For you, Jefe, always."

The men said goodbye, and Pablo immediately dialed Jack.

"How are you, Jack?"

"I'm good Pablo, we should arrive at the yard by noon. I've texted them our ETA."

"Be sure to ask for Juan, he has all the instructions and knows that I will be paying cash."

"What about the insurance?"

"There is no need for that, and if you make claims, then they raise your premiums. That industry is a criminal enterprise – they might as well just send bag men around the neighborhood to collect the money!"

Pablo laughed heartily at his own joke.

"Save the insurance for a time when I'm not around."

Jack hesitated as he sensed that another danger buoy just appeared in their relationship, but he shrugged it off.

"Ok, if that's how you wanna roll – it's your cash..." Jack trailed off and wondered where the cash had come from. He was already beginning to feel the weight.

"Jack, did I lose you?"

"No, sorry, something in front of us distracted me," he lied.

Lying was getting faster and easier, like a reflex.

"Okay. Anything else, my friend?" Pablo asked cordially.

"Yeah, I've got a lady on my crew, and I'd like to have her join us on the passage. She's got her shit wired tight: great sailor, decent cook, and good conversation. Plus, I get the feeling that she's hiding from someone, so she keeps a low profile."

"I can know a lot about someone when I look into their eyes. You will both join me for dinner tonight in Miami, I will decide then."

It was a command, not an invitation, and Jack felt the sting. Now, powerless, and penniless, he wondered, *How much of my soul am I trading for this money?*

9

Mariana sat at the helm and looked down at the last two tattoos she wanted to get rid of; she couldn't stand looking at them any longer. That life was over and reminders like the tattoos were unwanted visitors from the past that she preferred to avoid. *I'll have enough money to hit a tattoo shop in Fort Lauderdale. Why did I ever give a single shit about this ink? God, everything was so twisted up...*

She couldn't fathom how her sense of right and wrong had been so distorted - even though she knew exactly who was responsible for the distortion. Everything seemed so clear now that she had achieved a sense of balance and fluidity in the way that she moved through the world. But that was different from how she began her life.

The glance at her arm set her thoughts in motion. *Tall, goofy, white girl in a brown neighborhood – I couldn't have stood out more if I had tried. At least I know what it's like to experience prejudice. God, I just wanted acceptance, why is that always so complicated?*

The poor Latin neighborhood where she had grown up was dominated by several rival gangs. Mariana had been a bystander for most of her early life and ignored by the other kids. The gangs didn't want the heat. If something happened to a little white girl, it came with a twenty-four-seven news cycle until someone was behind bars. The news coverage of killed or missing Latinos was less enthusiastic. But as a young girl, being ignored may have been the worst part because it created a vacuum, and that emptiness would open a dark door in the summer before her freshman year of high school.

It began on a hot summer day in Miami after a heatwave had left the city on edge. She could hear horns honking and people arguing as she walked home from the community pool. As she passed the park, she saw two boys beating up a smaller boy that she knew from around the neighborhood. She had always been big for her age, and at nearly six feet tall, she was physically imposing with broad shoulders and toned muscles.

Mariana jumped into the fight without a second thought and pulled the attackers off by grabbing one in each hand and effortlessly tossing them on the ground. One of the boys got up and rushed at her blindly with his head down and was met with a hard strike to the skull that sent him face down into the dirt. The other boy finally worked up the courage to attack her by throwing a few punches that didn't land. She grabbed him by the throat with one hand while cocking the other like a piston, repeatedly ramming it into his nose before he dropped to the ground, bleeding, and gasping. Mariana's boxing lessons had paid off.

Seconds later, she had heard the screeching of tires and shouting in Spanish as three older boys came running up to the scene.

"Pobre niño!" said the boy's cousin as he picked the smaller boy up. Then, he looked at Mariana and asked, "Why did you help him?"

"I don't like bullies, and I don't like fights that aren't fair. It was two to one, so I just evened it out a little bit."

"And look, not a mark on you – so tough! I know you from around the neighborhood, Mariana, right?"

"Yeah, that's me. The white girl with the Spanish name who doesn't fit in with whites or browns."

"Well, now you can be as white or brown as you want to be. Do you know who you just saved?"

"No. I just know him from the block."

He called to the other boys, "Yo, she doesn't even know who she just rescued."

They all laughed.

He then turned to the boy who'd been beaten, "Let's take your new friend to meet your uncle, mijo. He's gonna want to thank her in person."

10

Windborne glided down the small canal that led to the boatyard entrance. Like most of the canals in the area, it was lined with beautiful homes and yachts tied off to private docks. Lush, green, tropical foliage surrounded them, and bright flowers punctuated the landscape. To Jack, the area seemed like the epicenter of the yachting universe. While he knew that he would be wrestling with the memory of Jen while he was in Fort Lauderdale, he was glad to be back in a place that at least felt like home. He looked out at a large iguana sitting on a dock and wondered if he had it better or worse than himself.

Jack was adding up the price of the houses and the huge yachts in front of them. He had rarely questioned his life choices until he lost Jen, now he questioned all of them. *I should just dive into this gangster thing. Then I could get a house on the canal with a private dock… How many of these were paid for by drug dealers, Ponzi schemes, lying stockbrokers? It's not the* honest, *hardworking guy that gets one of these – that guy gets screwed by the system.* For the first time in his life, his moral center was faltering, and it didn't bother him in the least.

Mariana came up from the saloon.

"Jack, can we talk a minute?"

"Sure, sit down," he replied as he patted the cockpit cushion next to him while continuing to pilot the boat down the narrow canal.

"I just wanted to see if you have any details, like how long is the boat going to be in the yard, will I get a half-day rate while we are on the hard, that kinda thing."

"I think it's going to take a month, and yeah, if my client approves of you, we can pay you. In fact, if that's the case, I'll pay you full rate – we'll have a lot of errands to do, and he's got a fat checkbook."

"Wow, that'd be fantastic. When do I meet him?"

"Tonight. We're going to have dinner with him. He's a really nice guy and I'm sure he's going to want you along for the ride."

"Super cool. I really appreciate it, Jack. I'm coming out of a bit of a tough spot myself."

"Maybe it's part of the plan," said Jack.

"What plan?" she asked.

"You know, *the* plan. People keep saying, it was meant to be, crap like that."

"I take it you're not a believer?" she asked.

"Not so much. How about you?"

"I've got what you might call foxhole religion. It was a term my uncle used about guys in combat that suddenly got religious. You know, like the guys that get hookers on liberty and then the Holy Ghost when the bullets start flying. He always thought they were hypocritical, but then some bad shit happened to me. Unbelievably bad. Suddenly I got religious. Maybe I'm a hypocrite, I don't know."

Jack contemplated her words. He had no such faith or the short-lived comfort it might bring.

"Well, there's no judgement on this boat. You can sort it when we're five-hundred miles offshore." He paused for a moment, and then said, "I wonder what it'd be like to believe that there's a point to all of this pointlessness?"

She shook her head in understanding, "I've got to believe there's something, the shit I've seen makes me *need* to believe."

"Well, let's hope that our storms are behind us Mariana. Maybe we've got nothin' but calm oceans and clear skies ahead. Let's hope anyway… We both need hope."

"I'll take that as an order, Cap. *Hope* it is." She looked ahead and said, "Hey, is that our yard?"

The boatyard came into view as they rounded a small bend in the canal.

"That's it," he answered.

Jack put the boat in neutral and stayed well off the docks while he called the number that Pablo had given him.

"This is Juan," said the man who answered the phone.

"Hey, this is Jack Kelly with *Windborne,* we are out in front of you on the canal, which lane would you like me in?"

"Hold on one second, Jack."

Jack expertly held the yacht in place, pointing her into the wind and current with just enough throttle and helm to hold it steady.

"Center lane, come on in," said Juan.

"Roger," was all that Jack said as he hung up the phone.

"Which side, Skipper, port or starboard?"

"Lines on port if you please, Ms. Hansen."

He'd phrased the order like a 19th century British Naval Officer. The Napoleonic wars era was his favorite period of nautical history.

She got the reference and smiled, responding with an attempt at a British accent, "Aye, Cap'n."

She made her way forward and took out three dock lines and fenders from the forward gear locker. As she was tying them to the twisted damaged stanchions, she said, "It looks like the wind is going to blow us off – stern spring line?"

"Yeah, that's what I'm thinking. The bow thruster is still not working."

Jack brought the port stern of the boat up to the dock, and she tossed the rearmost line down onto the dock cleat and flipped it back on itself taking another wrap on the cleat. Mariana then checked to ensure that a fender was between the stern and the dock, turned her head to Jack and nodded up to indicate that they were ready to spring the boat. Jack pushed the throttle forward and the tension was taken up on the stern line. Once it was taught, the boat sprung forward and against the dock. He left the engine in forward as she stepped off to tie off the bow and amidships line.

"All good Cap," came the call from the dock as she made all three lines fast and well.

Jack shifted to neutral and pushed the stop button on the engine panel. Then, he went down below to grab his paperwork. When he came up, there was a man standing in the cockpit.

"Hello Jack, I'm Juan," he said with a warm smile.

"Nice to meet you, here's all my paperwork," Jack said as he handed him the boat's documentation and insurance.

"We won't need any of this," said Juan, "Everything is taken care of my friend."

"Is Pablo sure he doesn't want to use the insurance?"

"He doesn't like to attract any attention to himself, you know? And, when his mind is made up, there is no changing it. Do you understand this?"

Jack nodded, seemingly in understanding, but the question mark in his mind grew much larger.

"We're going to be working nearly around the clock, so I've arranged a nearby vacation rental and loaner car for you and your mate. It's only a few blocks away." Juan paused to pull the keys out of his pocket. "Here you go, I'll drop a map pin and text you. There's a store and some restaurants right down the street." He pointed toward the north end of the yard. "You have my cell if you need anything at all. We'll start work on the boat today."

"Ok, sounds like a plan."

Jack fished through his papers, and pulled out a handwritten list, handing it to Juan.

"Here's my list, but she needs a surveyor to do a full inspection, can you arrange that too?"

“Yes, anything my friend. Why don’t you take a few minutes for you and your mate to gather your things while we prepare the straps and crane for the hoist.”

“Ok,” he said to Juan. Then he shouted, “Mariana, up here please.”

“Just a sec, Jack,” she called back.

When Mariana came up, he reviewed everything with her. Then they went below and assembled their duffle bags.

Jack’s bag included a good stack of Jen’s pictures and a bottle of his best rum. He wasn’t sure how he felt about leaving the boat. *Will I sleep better or worse?* He tossed a copy of *The Old Man and the Sea* on top of his gear, zipped the bag shut and threw it over his shoulder.

It didn’t take Mariana long to pack because she had been living out of a duffle bag for years. After her few articles of clothes and toiletries were packed, she threw in the only personal article in her possession - a very expensive, jewel studded dagger.

11

Jack and Mariana got cleaned up and ready for dinner with Pablo. As they waited for the car, Jack could tell that she was nervous.

"Once he meets you, I'm sure he's going to want you onboard."

"Job interviews wind me up a bit."

"Think of it less of an interview and more of a meet and greet," Jack said.

"What does he do for a living?" Mariana asked.

"I'm not really sure – some kind of business conglomerate. He doesn't talk much about his work."

The two sailors waited silently for a few moments outside the house. Both of them were nervous for vastly different reasons. She was nervous about being so close to Miami for the next month – although she was excited to sneak in a visit with her mom. He was nervous about his new relationship with Pablo. It was also bothering him that he was starting to have feelings for Mariana, but like everything else in his life, he cared less with every passing day. There was little space remaining in his mind to evaluate right from wrong. For better or for worse, the Captain was living in the moment.

The town car picked them up promptly at 7:15 PM and they settled in for the forty-five-minute drive to the restaurant. After a few moments of silence, Mariana asked Jack, "How do you feel when you're doing it?" Mariana asked.

Jack, surprised and amused by the phrasing, smiled at her, and answered, "I feel good when I do it, don't you?"

She realized what she had said as they both laughed.

"Sorry, in my mind that was a super-complete question. What I meant was, when you're running the boat – working as a captain – how do you feel?"

"Like I belong there. Like I don't have to try to fit in with all the other kids at school. It's a natural feeling, at least it *was* a natural feeling. I don't know how I'll feel on this run." Then, softening his tone as if to underscore the gravity about what he was about to say, he continued, "I sure as hell don't know how I'm going to feel if I ever get my license back. You know, I didn't ask you if you were ok being on this Colombia trip even though my license was pulled – I'll be breaking a few laws."

"I'm sure it would take you a while to catch up to me on the law-breaking. No, that's not a problem for me, but thanks for asking."

They sat silently for a few minutes before Mariana spoke again.

"Jack, I've watched you carefully over the last two weeks. Other than zoning out and almost ramming into that dredge – I'd say you're damn good at all of it – especially the people part. I've worked for some captains that were such assholes, they should only be licensed to work without a crew."

Jack considered her words as they both drifted back into silence and looked out the windows toward the brightly lit city in the distance. *Eventually I will have to answer the question as to my fitness for duty,* he thought. *Whatever it ends up being, I'll give them a straight answer. No bullshit.*

"What'd you do before this?" Jack asked her.

"I was involved in some activities that can lead to orange jumpsuits – can we just leave it at that?"

Jack nodded, understanding the code of the maritime crew community. Many wanted, or needed, silence and a low profile. *It's been that way for a thousand years; people leaving shore to escape something on shore. I'm certainly no different.*

After a brief pause, she continued.

"I mean, I'm not a serial killer or anything like that," she said, smiling at him.

"Well, that's good, because I know guys on a long passage that would kill for a bowl of cereal with fresh milk – true cereal killers."

She shook her head in mocking disapproval at his attempt at humor as he chuckled softly at his own joke.

"If you're gonna crack jokes like that all the way, I may have to rethink this."

They smiled at each other, appreciating a few light moments in their otherwise heavy worlds.

What about you?" she asked.

"Me and Jen did day work in Fort Lauderdale for a few years to put enough away to start the business. I bounced around before that in Southern Cali, but nothing ever stuck. My mom said there was a time when you could live a good, middle-class life in Southern California. A working guy - like a cop - could afford a house and a small boat. Then it started to change; it got really expensive, and fast. I knew I'd never keep up, but the final straw was a bad breakup. It sent me across the country to start over, and that's how I met Jen."

"The shit we do for love," was all that Mariana said as she looked back out the window. Her tone contained a depth of understanding in her soul, mixed with more than a little disgust.

Jack caught it and skipped his next question, silently looking back out the window at the night sky.

The time passed quickly, and soon they were combing their way through busy streets to the waterside restaurant. The driver pulled up to the valet stand, stepped out and opened the door for them. He handed Jack a card with his number.

"Text me five minutes before you're ready, and I'll be waiting right here," said the driver.

Jack started to reach into his wallet for a tip and the driver shook his head and said, "It's all taken care of sir, tip and everything."

"Thank you," Jack said as he and Mariana turned away to walk into the very high-end establishment.

"I suddenly feel underdressed," said Mariana as she glanced around at the elite crowd.

"Yeah, me too," Jack responded, then turning to the hostess, "We're here to meet-" Jack was interrupted by Pablo who had appeared quietly behind them.

"They are here to meet me," Pablo said enthusiastically.

Then he took three slow deliberate steps toward them, exclaiming, "Mariana! This is a miracle!"

"You two know each other? Does that mean she's in?" Jack asked.

"Yes, yes, of course she is! Gloria a Dios!" Pablo shouted as he threw his arms around her.

Jack looked at Mariana, expecting to see a smile on her face because Pablo approved. Instead, he saw a look of sheer terror.

"I asked God for your return each day!"

"Hello, Pablo," she said dryly and without emotion.

Pablo and Mariana stared at each other in silence as Jack began to contemplate what had just happened.

The hostess mercifully interrupted the silence.

"Your table is ready, right this way."

The three of them went off to what would prove to be an awkward reunion dinner that would leave Jack feeling like he was having dinner alone.

Pablo had always held Mariana close to his heart, for he knew that he would not have children of his own. She was the daughter that he had never had, and she had run far and fast to escape the man that she had once called papa.

12

Windborne had been in the yard for ten days and the progress was easy to see. The stump of a mast was gone, the deck had been stripped, painted, and garnished with bright stainless-steel hardware. The stanchions which had been grossly disfigured by the big wave had been replaced, and new stainless lifelines surrounded the boat. Today, the new mast was being stepped. A huge crane on shore would lift the mast into place before a team of riggers would take over, working their way up, down, and around the mast like spiders, carefully installing and tensioning the standing rigging cables that would hold it in place.

Jack walked over to Juan and handed him a coin, saying, “Here’s the coin for good luck.”

Juan turned the coin over in his hands and looked at it carefully, and then said, “It is very beautiful – solid gold?”

“Sure is, from the Atocha.”

Jack was referring to the shipwreck of *Nuestra Señora de Atocha,* which sank off of Marquesas Key about 20 miles from Key West. She went down with forty tons of gold and silver and almost seventy pounds of emeralds mined in Colombia.

"¡Dios mio! Do you think it's a good idea to have a coin from a shipwreck on your sailboat?"

"I'd say a coin that laid on the ocean floor from 1622 until 1985 and then eventually found its way to me, belongs on my sailboat. Plus, as you have seen the evidence, the ocean has already tried to kill me. What've I got to lose?"

"As you wish, my friend, as you wish. I will personally place it under the mast."

The tradition was known to go all the way back to Roman times and thought to be a means of payment to enter the afterlife and potentially to bring luck. Juan walked away seemingly unconvinced that this was a good idea, and that perhaps it would even bring bad luck. Mariners are a very superstitious bunch and for good reason - sometimes, luck is all you have on the ocean and Jack Kelly had seen damn little of it.

After Jack was satisfied with the progress at the yard, he and Mariana made their way along the canal to *Grind it Right* for an espresso and croissant. There was a heavy mist in the air that morning, creating an eerie setting as it lay on the water. The two of them sat quietly, sipping espresso, and looking out over the canal.

Jack had noticed that Mariana had not seemed herself since she'd been reunited with Pablo. She had also deliberately avoided giving him any details about their previous relationship. Twice he had tried to pry, but then backed off. Whatever it was, it certainly wasn't good. The conversation between her and Pablo at the dinner largely centered around what she had been doing since she left Miami. Pablo wanted all of the details and seemed to take a genuine interest in her life. They had acted cordially enough in front of Jack, but the tension in the air had been thick enough to taste, and it had tasted rancid.

Mariana stared into the distance, deliberately avoiding eye contact with Jack, and said, "I heard Juan say something yesterday."

"Yeah, what's that?" he replied sleepily and somewhat disinterested.

"He told one of his workers to, 'Double glass an aft compartment and add mounts for two more life rafts in the garage,'" she said. "They didn't realize that I had come down below - it was one of the few times I didn't hit my head."

Jack's face turned red, and he started firing off questions. "Two more life rafts? Why would we need three life rafts? And what the hell is getting double glassed? I don't like the sound of any of this – how well do you know Pablo?"

She replied tersely, "Don't make this conversation about me and Pablo. This is about *you* and *Windborne.*"

"Fair enough," was all he said to her as he sat and stewed in this revelation. Then his anger flashed without warning, and he snapped, "You should've said something yesterday."

The conversation ended as awkwardly as it had begun. They both returned to staring out the window again as if in the distance, one or both of them would find solitude. Their gaze was transfixed on nothing, but it was somewhere to hide.

After a few minutes of contemplation, Jack said, "I'll get into it with Juan at the yard."

"I wouldn't," was all that she offered.

Again, the silence.

After twenty minutes of staring out the window without saying a word, Jack nodded to indicate that it was time to go, so they left the coffee shop and walked back to the yard.

When they arrived, Jack caught a whiff of the morning cocktail of paint, solvent, new canvas, and saltwater. He breathed it in deeply. For a brief moment the aromas transported him to the simplicity of his youth in Dana Point Harbor 2,700 miles to the west; a distance that felt like a million miles from where he stood at that moment.

They could see that Juan was directing a large lift with a boat in its slings.

"Take it back to the corner so the paint shop can tent her," he shouted over the thumping of the giant crane's engine.

Jack waited for a minute, not wanting to interrupt the operation underway, and Mariana continued walking over to *Windborne*. After the crane had stopped moving, Jack approached him saying, "Hey, Juan. I have a few questions for you."

"Got you, Jack. I'll meet you by *Windborne* in a couple of minutes."

Jack nodded and walked over to join Mariana at the side of his boat.

Mariana looked at him as if nothing out of the ordinary had just happened between them, and said, "She's looking hella good Jack."

To Mariana, the tension between her and Jack wasn't even on the scale; she was used to far worse.

"Yeah. She looks even better than when we first bought her. It sure is nice having a big wallet at a boatyard."

"You think that now, but everything comes with a cost. The price that he asks you to pay is loyalty. It's too expensive," she said with a serious, solemn look on her face.

"Mariana, come on. You've got to tell me what you know."

"Anything I tell you becomes a weight for you *and* for me."

"If it's that bad, why don't you just take off?"

"You don't get it, Jack. We both work for him now. You don't get to just walk away. Didn't you realize what you were getting into?"

"It crossed my mind, but I pushed it out pretty fast," Jack said.

"Why did you push it out?"

Jack rubbed his head with both hands and stared off into the distance. Then finally, he answered her, "I guess there are a lot of reasons, but at the top of that list is that I just don't care anymore. I wanted my boat fixed as fast as possible so that I could sail far away. Pablo is nothing more than a means to an end for me, and if I have to cross a few lines to get there, so be it."

"A few lines? You have no idea what you have gotten yourself into, Jack Kelly."

A loud beeping alerted them to a lift crane's movement; they re-positioned themselves, allowing it to pass safely.

"Jack," Juan called as he walked up to them.

"Juan, tell me about the double-glassed compartments and extra life rafts," Jack asked with the knife-edge tone of a prosecutor.

Juan was clearly taken off guard and tried to quickly regain his composure.

"Safety, of course, my friend. What else?"

"I don't know what else, you tell me."

"Pablo was concerned for your safety, so we added a few water-tight compartments, and a crash wall, along with two additional life rafts."

Jack knew that the answer barely passed for plausible, but he shook it off. His ability to care about rules had suddenly slid off a cliff. *Fuck it,* he thought.

"Ok, sounds good. You should run any other changes by me first," Jack said in a more congenial tone.

"Sure, Jack. I've gotta get another boat started on her re-fit. We good here?"

"Yeah, we're good. Thanks, Juan."

After Juan was out of earshot, Mariana chimed back in, "That's complete bullshit, you realize that don't you?"

"At some level."

"At all levels, Jack. We are now part of a criminal enterprise, one that I tried pretty hard to escape. Now, I'm back in it. The only difference is that I'm going to be stuck on a sailboat with Pablo. This is fucking perfect."

"You should just leave. I'll give you some money for a flight, just get the hell out of here. This is my vortex of shit pulling you in."

"You don't just leave Pablo. Nobody does."

"You did it once, do it again."

"For some reason, he has forgiven me for leaving the first time, I don't think that he'll be so generous the second time around. Have you ever heard the term, *blood in, blood out?"*

"Yeah, I've heard it. Is that a real thing?"

"Very real, Jack. Plus, do you fight with the universe much?"

"Huh?"

"Do you fight with the universe?"

"I don't think so, why?"

"Well, I spent three years, running, hiding, and learning a new trade on the water, and the universe dropped me at the dinner table of the very man I was running from. Is that a fight that I can win?"

"What are we supposed to do, just accept the shit as it lands on us?" Jack asked incredulously.

"Isn't that what you have been doing for the last four months? The universe dumped you in the same bucket of shit that I was trying to crawl out of, don't act like you're not somehow part of this."

"Hey, piss off! You got on the boat, no one put a gun to your head," Jack said harshly.

"A gun to my head? That's actually a perfect idiom, Jack. If you only knew..." She broke eye contact and looked away from Jack's intense glare.

“Get the fuck off if you don’t like the course. That’s the way boat life works Mariana, you get on boats you like, and get off ones you don’t like. It’s not complicated.”

Mariana tried to hide the tears forming in her eyes. This was a side of Jack she hadn’t seen, one that she could barely believe existed.

She changed the subject.

“It’s hard to imagine the force it took to flip the boat and snap the mast like a toothpick,” said Mariana.

He shook his head, saying, “It happened so fast, I mean, one second you realize you’re upside down, then right side up, then she’s gone...” Jack’s voice trailed off.

Mariana didn’t pry when Jack stopped talking. Both of them had memories better left unspoken. She was tired of running and hiding. On the surface, she had painfully accepted that her fight with fate was over. Underneath the surface, in the dark recesses of her mind, she was not entirely ungrateful to be back in the fold. She was conditioned to believe that was where she belonged - with family.

13

Jack's moral compass was swinging wildly. Pablo's effect on him had been one of a strong, vacillating magnetic field. Jack was no longer able to find his true north. Everything pointed south.

"I wish I was able to talk to you, Babe," Jack said aloud to the ghost that traveled with him. "I know you'd be able to help me sort this."

Who else can I talk to? Mariana? No, her perspective would be skewed because of her connection with Pablo. Mom? I can't bear it… Brett? Yeah, definitely Brett.

Captain Brett was a friend of Jack's from the super-yacht circuit. He'd started working with Jack when they were both deck hands, and quickly worked his way up the ranks. Now, he was working as the captain on a celebrity owned, twenty-million dollar, 125' Motor Yacht.

Jack pulled out his cell phone and searched for the number, then hit the call button. A soft-spoken man with an Australian accent answered the phone.

"Jack, How the hell are ya, mate?"

"Hey Brett, long time, eh? Where are you these days?"

"Yeah, it's been a minute for sure. I'm over in Corfu, Greece waiting for the boss to show up."

"How long you been waiting?"

"'Bout a month. Every day it's the same old routine: get the crew washing, polishing, repairs, blah, blah. We're all losing our minds waiting, waiting, waiting."

"That's part of the gig," Jack said in an understanding tone.

"Yeah, for sure, Bro."

"But they make up for it in the pay, right?"

"They do, and the owners buy my beer, so I guess I shouldn't be complaining."

"The crosses we bear as captains," Jack quipped.

Brett chuckled, and then in a serious tone, he said, "Hey, I heard from someone that you nearly lost *Windborne.* Tell me that's a bad rumor, mate."

"Naw, man, it's the truth. Jen's dead, Brett. And they pulled my ticket."

"Jesus, I'm so sorry to hear that, Bro. Anything I can do?"

"I need some advice, or at least a sounding board if you don't mind."

"All right, give it a go."

Jack laid out the state of the boat, his initial plans to work in Fort Lauderdale, the call from Pablo and the trip to Colombia. He knew he'd get the nod of approval from Brett. Jack needed an enabler and Brett was his first call because he didn't mind bending boundaries.

"Yeah, sounds a bit off, mate. But it's a hell of a deal – I'd take the money and run if I were you."

"I don't know… None of it makes sense. Why would the guy want to take the long route on a sailboat, when he can certainly afford a ride like yours?" Jack said.

"Why don't you ask yourself the same question?"

"Huh?"

Brett asked the implied question, "You don't think it's odd that you are perfectly happy crossing an ocean at a snail's pace, but you think it's odd that *he* wants to do it?"

"Good point."

The men remained silent for a few moments while Brett's message settled into Jack's mind.

Jack continued, "My mind is in a dark place, my friend. I'm just coloring everything I see with that darkness. I feel like I've lost the ability to see good. Honestly, it scares me a bit. Ya know, I actually thought to myself, 'What the hell, if he's doing something illegal, why should I care?'"

"That's a fair question, why should you care?"

"I don't know, laws, prisons? I guess you could say I have an aversion to confined spaces."

"Fair enough," was all the Aussie said.

"Sorry to lay this on you, I just don't have anyone to talk to about it, and I feel like I'm losing my way."

"Look, mate. Do it, don't do it, it doesn't matter. I can tell you with a degree of certainty that Captain Jack Kelly will *always* find his way. You've got a good heart, Bro, and that will keep you on the right path."

"I appreciate that, man. More than you can know."

"Jack, I'm standing at the bridge watching two of my deckhands screaming at each other – might come to blows – I gotta bounce."

"Yeah, go get 'em, mate," said Jack.

"Cheers," replied Brett as he hung up the phone.

Brett had a reason to trust Jack Kelly's character. Besides the time they had spent together at sea, he had seen Jack's friendship in action. He had said to Jack on more than one occasion, "You're one of the good ones," noting how Jack stood by him through good times and bad. But the Captain Jack Kelly that Brett had known was not the same man with whom he had just spoken.

Jack looked down at the phone in his hand and again thought about calling his mom but decided against it. As he sat on the edge of the floating dock with his feet in the water, the reality of his situation began to catch up with him. *It's too late to set a new course. The money has changed hands. What do I think I'm going to do, walk up to Pablo and tell him that I changed my mind after he spent all that money on Windborne? And what would he say, 'Sure, no problem, Jack. We'll work out a payment plan.' Shit, I'm living in an imaginary world even considering this.* He knew that Pablo wouldn't take 'no' for an answer.

Jack put his phone down with the solemn realization that his morals had been bought for the price of a re-fitted sailboat. It hardly seemed like a fair price to the desperate man.

14

Jack and Pablo sat together at a small café off the canal, with several large charts laid out on the table that were held in place by half-eaten plates of food and coffee cups.

Jack began the briefing, “Looks like our best route will be to sail east-northeast, out to around 27° north, and 66° west - that’s north and east of the Bahamas. Once we get to 66° - that’s the meridian of Puerto Rico,” he pointed at the chart, “we’ll make our turn to the south. After that we can expect to pick up the northeasterly trades and ride them down to Puerto Rico and then on to Colombia.”

Pablo nodded in approval, and said, “I would like to stop and see someone in San Juan.”

“That works.”

Jack picked up a mechanical pencil and an eighteen-inch parallel ruler and began to plot a course line from Fort Lauderdale to the turn point, and then he drew a line down to intersect with Puerto Rico. He then walked the parallel ruler from the course lines to the nearest compass rose and took the readings, then wrote down some course notes on the chart.

Jack took a deep breath and let it out slowly as he rolled up the charts.

"All right, that looks good. I'm a little nervous because the boat work was completed so fast – it won't even be mid-November when we leave."

"I've lived here for many years Jack; I've never seen anything significant develop this close to the end of hurricane season."

"You don't know what it's like out there when it gets bad – I do. Not to mention, I haven't had good luck with the normal patterns." There was an unusual edge in Jack's voice.

"Jack, we'll be fine. Let's talk about women and dancing in Colombia to set your mind on something more pleasant," he said, reaching over to touch Jack's hand in reassurance. A gesture that seemed uncharacteristic of who Jack believed Pablo to be.

Jack sighed in surrender and nodded his head. *It almost doesn't matter what I want anymore; I work for Pablo. Maybe the universe has a plan that includes me dying at sea... Who the hell knows? Fatalism it is...*

Pablo interrupted Jack's thoughts, "I spoke with Juan today, and you are clear to start provisioning *Windborne.* Provision for four people please."

Jack pointed to Pablo, "One," then to himself, "two," then said, "Mariana is three. Who's the fourth?"

"My personal security, he's sitting in the booth behind you, would you like to meet him?" He motioned for the man to come over and sit down.

"Jack, this is Diego. You have actually been just feet from him on several occasions, but he is skilled at blending in and disappearing."

Jack reached across the table to shake hands with the big, muscular man. He noticed the scar jutting out from under his mustache on the left side of his face. As Diego extended his hand, Jack saw the tattoo on his wrist - it was the same as Mariana's.

"Welcome to the *Windborne* crew, Diego. It's nice to meet you."

Diego managed a small smile and shook Jack's hand with such firmness that Jack almost recoiled.

"Well, I guess we're down to the most important questions, what do you like to eat and drink?"

At Jack's comment, the mood seemed to lighten for all three of them, as they all smiled and began discussing meals, snacks, and drinks.

"I, of course, as your captain, will not be drinking underway."

"This is nonsense my friend. I insist that you will have a drink with me each afternoon," said Pablo, "You are too serious."

Jack thought about it. Then he thought about how carefully he'd been following the rules. Everything he'd done to get his license, all of the hard work, all of the sacrifice. It all added up to nothing when it came to saving Jen.

"You're right Pablo, I am too damned serious. Okay then, drinks at sunset per the request of the primary charter guest. Done."

Diego asked Pablo a question in Spanish.

Jack thought, *Here's a guy that probably never followed a rule, and he could buy and sell me ten times over without even noticing a change in his bank statement. I've been a sucker my whole life.*

"Jack, I hope you don't mind, but I had your satellite upgraded. It will allow us to stay up on things while we are offshore."

"Thank you, Pablo. I don't mind at all," Jack said with a smile.

The server laid the check down and Pablo picked it up.

"Anything else?" Pablo asked them and was answered with slow, contemplative, shaking heads.

Jack thought carefully before he said anything, but no matter how hard he tried, he couldn't keep his mouth shut.

"Pablo, what's the deal with the sealed compartments – do I even want to know?"

"Juan suggested these were good safety measures. I didn't think you would mind given all that you had been through."

"So, you don't have anything stashed in there?"

"Jack, you worry too much. We will work on this - Colombia will wear off on you – I promise! A new, relaxed, and happier Jack Kelly will return to the States."

Jack knew that the answer was bullshit. *To hell with it. Here we go.* Then he said, "I guess Colombia will be the medicine that the doctor ordered."

The three men stood up and Pablo dropped a fifty-dollar bill on the table to pay for a twenty-dollar breakfast. *Money to burn,* thought Jack. *That's a better way to live.*

15

On the morning of Pablo's 16th birthday, his father sat him down at the table to reveal that for one of his birthday gifts, he would be joining a new club. Killing was the price of admission. Pablo had waited eagerly for this day since he was a young boy.

"Son, there is a rival that is causing problems for our family. Today, I will kill him and his lieutenants. You will kill his son."

The teen nodded in understanding.

"I don't like to kill children. You understand this, yes?"

"Yes, Don."

He had stopped calling him father around fourteen, hearing the other men call him, "Don," and he wanted desperately to be one of his father's men.

"Remember the lesson you learned when you beat that boy?"

"Yes, I should have killed him, or he might've come back to harm mama or my sisters."

"Yes, that is right my son!"

"I will kill him with my bare hands!" Pablo said and raised his hands as if he were choking someone. His father was amused and smiled at him, which was something he rarely did.

"That won't be necessary. I've placed a .45 caliber pistol in your lunchbox - just like the one we used when I taught you to shoot. It is brand new, with mother of pearl hand grips. It is incredibly beautiful, and the pistol is your birthday present. There is a round in the chamber; it has double action so you will only need to pull the trigger – you remember how it works?"

"Yes, Don."

"You will kill him at lunchtime at exactly 12:15 - and you will tell no one of this plan - especially your mother!"

"I understand, Don."

Children were arriving at the school from all directions like ants on a pile of sugar in chaos and order at the same time. Pablo took his usual path, making his way to his first classroom of the day. It was like any other day, except that on this day, one life would end in death, and another would be re-born into a life of death and darkness.

Pablo was willing to do anything to earn his father's approval, and he didn't care who had to suffer. Like the good foot-soldier that he was becoming, he followed the orders carefully. Throughout the day, he acted normally and waited for lunch. Once he was in the cafeteria, he found the boy sitting alone and sat behind him. At the appointed time, Pablo opened his lunchbox under the table and took out the pistol. He could feel the cold steel in his hand, and the weight of the gun told him that he had a full magazine - his father had trained him well. He remembered that his father had cautioned him, “Make sure that the angle of your shot is down or toward a solid object, we don’t want to harm the other children.” Pablo assessed the angle, tucked the gun under his shirt, and walked up behind the boy. He didn’t think about the boy’s father being killed today, nor did he have any concern for the boy’s mother, who would lose both a husband and a son. He only thought about one thing, *Do this well so that Papa will be proud*.

He pulled the gun from under his shirt, placed it on the boy’s head, and said, “Today you die.” Then pulling the trigger, he watched the boy’s head explode out the front onto the lunch table as the other children screamed and ran for cover. The hollow-point bullet had done its work, and Pablo calmly dropped the hammer to its resting position and tucked the gun under his belt. He would carry this gun for the rest of his life.

A teacher who had seen the execution went to the headmaster of the school.

“It was Don Julio’s boy.”

The men looked gravely at each other and stood in awkward silence.

The headmaster responded with defeat in his voice, “Then nothing can be done. Bring the boy to me.”

Pablo was asked to speak with the headmaster in his office.

"Pablo, why did you do this?"

"I had orders. Men follow orders."

"Good men do not kill innocent boys, Pablo. That is not how we have taught you to live."

"I don't need you, or this place. I am the son of Don Julio!" he slammed his fist on the desk.

The headmaster reminded himself that the boy was still armed.

"Then we will part with an understanding, and on good terms. This is not a matter for the police. You are free to go, but it is my hope that you will choose not to return."

"Goodbye then," Pablo said as he stood and walked out of the office, leaving behind his backpack, books, and lunchbox. He left with the only possession that mattered, *his* pistol. His most prized of all possessions, for with it had come his father's affection.

16

Windborne floated peacefully in a temporary slip at the boatyard. She looked majestic. The hull was painted a deep, navy blue, with a gold boot stripe at the waterline. All of the teak was brightly varnished, adding warmth to the yacht. Jack noticed something different about the lettering of the boat's name; it looked *very* gold. He leaned over the edge of the stern to inspect it more closely. Then, he turned over his shoulder to Pablo and asked, "Gold?"

"Yes, my friend, I had it done with real gold in the paint."

"Holy crap, that looks amazing, thank you Pablo."

"Well, now you can charge more for your charters!" Pablo said with a hearty laugh.

Mariana shook her head in disgust as she overheard the conversation. Diego took note of her response. She'd almost thrown up when she saw Diego. She knew what he was and wanted no part of him or Pablo. *Yet here I am,* she thought to herself.

Jack invited them all to sit down for a short briefing.

"All right everyone, this is your last chance for a few weeks to stretch your legs on shore. We need to go checkout at customs, and we could stop at the store if you forgot any personal items or special snacks."

They smiled and nodded.

Pablo interrupted the briefing.

"Diego and I will not be checking out – we prefer to maintain a low profile."

The four of them sat in silence as Jack took this in. It was another indication of the unrevealed nature of their journey.

"Okay, Pablo, that's your call. Mariana and I will drive to customs."

The customs agency in Fort Lauderdale was a twenty-minute drive from where they were located. The whole system operated on good faith. Boats came and went twenty-four hours a day and were supposed to check in and out of customs. The odds were in your favor that no one would ever inspect your boat unless you seemed suspicious, or they happened to bump into the needle in the haystack.

Pablo said, "Do me a favor Jack, pick me up a bottle of fifty-year-old Tawny Port at Edgewater Specialty up on Birch."

He pulled out a wad of cash, removed the fat rubber band holding it together, and peeled off five, crisp, one-hundred-dollar bills. Jack noticed that the entire stack was hundreds. He couldn't fathom how much cash was in the man's pocket.

"Sure thing, Boss. Anything for you, Pablo."

The normally silent man, remained so, and shook his head.

"Mariana, do you have your passport?"

She flashed it with a shitty smile. Diego noted that too – he was watching her closely. He was by nature and necessity a man that was distrustful, and she had earned his distrust by running away. *The bitch doesn't deserve to wear that crest, I should cut it off of her!* He happily would have done it, if not for the fact that he knew she was under Pablo's protection.

Jack started to get up and said, "We should be gone no more than a few hours. You've got my cell if you need it."

Pablo raised a finger and said, "Maybe now, Diego?"

Diego nodded.

Pablo said, "Jack, may I see your phone? And yours too Mariana."

Though they were perplexed and startled by the request, they complied. For Mariana knew what Jack was learning: Pablo's instructions and "requests" were to be followed without question.

"Are these backed up to the cloud?"

Jack said, "Yeah, mine is – recently."

Mariana said, "Me too."

"Bueno," said Pablo as he handed them to Diego.

Diego took the phones over to the edge of the boat and dropped them in the canal.

"What the fuck!" Jack shouted.

Mariana knew better.

Pablo said calmly, "Jack, you may ask me many things, which I will patiently answer." Then he took two steps toward the Captain and stood just inches from him, while Jack watched Pablo's face transform into a raging storm. "You may ask, but you will ALWAYS DO SO POLITELY," he screamed the last words as he pounded his fist down on the sailboat's roof to punctuate his sentence.

Jack recoiled and took a step back. The four of them stood in silence while Pablo adjusted his clothing as if this upset had somehow ruffled his garments.

Finally, Pablo said in a warm inviting tone, "Now, enough of this unpleasantness! We have a cruise; this is our destiny! Good times for all, this is what I want the most!"

As if it were a different person speaking, he smiled and patted Jack on the shoulder, then gave Mariana a half hug saying, "My dear prodigal daughter has returned, and for this I am so grateful."

Mariana tried to manage a smile. She knew the rules: Display fear when necessary and show happiness and gratitude when that's what he wanted to see. To be in Pablo's orbit was to have *his* gravity control one's own emotions. Jack did not yet know the rules, and Mariana made a mental note to review them with him. She had learned many of them the hard way. Pablo's anger was well worth avoiding.

Diego, unnoticed, had disappeared below and was now reappearing with a phone in his hand which he handed to Pablo.

Pablo handed the phone to Jack and said, "Here, use this one today if you need to contact me or make any calls. My number is in there under, Boss. Give it to Diego when you return. I'll buy you both brand new phones after the trip."

Jack responded, "Ok, Boss." The word that Pablo had used to indicate his location in the contacts on the burner phone. The title that Jack had already used a few times. It was a word that no longer felt strange or foreign on Jack's lips. When Mariana heard this change in Jack's tone, her heart sank.

Jack checked his pocket for his passport before saying in a somewhat annoyed tone, "I can't call for a car now, because the app was on my phone."

"No apps, too much surveillance. I knew you would need a car. Pablo pulled out his phone and dialed.

"Juan," was all he said when his call was answered.

"Yes, Jefe."

"Jack needs your car for a few hours."

"I'll meet him at the top of the ramp," he answered subserviently.

"Right away," Pablo said sternly.

"Of course, Jefe!" Juan said with great urgency.

Pablo turned back to them saying, "See, I take care of everything, and you worry about nothing."

He smiled warmly and patted them on the back as they stepped toward the dock.

"Jefe," Jack called from the dock.

Surprised and delighted to hear Jack say 'boss' in Spanish, he smiled and said, "Yes, my son."

"Do you enjoy good cigars?"

"Yes, please get some of those too."

Pablo started to reach for his wad of cash, but Jack waved him off.

"No, these will be my gift to you. For all of your generosity, Don Pablo."

There it was. Mariana had seen it dozens of times in others. She felt her chest constrict as she watched a man whom she thought to be moral, surrender so easily to a man she knew to be so immoral. Pablo had bought Jack for a little over $100,000. She desperately wanted to judge him, but she could not. Her price had been even lower, an ice cream cone on a hot day, and the fatherly love of a charismatic man that she admired. She forced a small amount of bile in her mouth back down her throat and stepped off the boat. Now, she would complete her tasks just like the good soldier that Pablo had come to rely on in the past.

17

Jack and Mariana drove in complete silence, each lost in a tumultuous world of thought driven by Pablo, storms, death, loss, and questions about the nature of free will. Jack was laser focused on the road and held onto the steering wheel tightly, as if it were the helm of *Windborne* on that fateful night. Mariana leaned her head on the window as if the strain of holding it upright was simply too much for her to bear. After a tense twenty minutes, they finally arrived at customs to check out of the country.

Jack and Mariana entered the nondescript government building, erected during a time when there were still people in government concerned about how taxpayer money was being spent. No frills, no updates, just clean and serviceable, with a faint smell of an industrial cleaning solution. They waited patiently and quietly in line and had not spoken to each other since leaving the dock. Perhaps the gravity of the crimes they were about to commit was stifling their speech.

When they were called forward to the window, a short, heavyset woman in a Customs Border Patrol uniform looked at them sternly, as if she possessed the ability to see into their souls. Had that actually been the case, she would have recoiled in shock, seeing the darkness and agony inside of them. She saw only the outside, and the layers underneath concealed the dark truth.

The agent took the CBP 1300 form and looked at it carefully. Box 8 said that Jack Kelly was the owner of the vessel; Jack had wondered if this was really true anymore given his new relationship with Pablo. Box 15 listed the ports of call; Colombia was not on the list. Box 16 "Cargo" was marked N/A, they were a pleasure craft – no cargo on board. Another lie. Title 18 section 1001 had been violated. Jack had just committed his first felony in lying to an agent of the government; how many more would follow?

Jack continued answering the agent's scripted questions. Yes, they were traveling on pleasure. Where? Mostly just island hopping in the Caribbean. White sandy beaches and palm trees were mentioned with enthusiastic smiles. The agent asked if they would enjoy some nice tropical rum drinks. Yes, they told her they would drink too much rum. Married? No, just a casual relationship.

The lonely agent looked Jack up and down a few times as if she might eat him. Then, she would glance disdainfully at the tall, fit, young woman that stood next to him. *Whore,* she thought to herself. *Screwing a guy to get a ride on his yacht – I'm sure mom and dad would be proud.* She couldn't have been further from the truth. Had she known all that Mariana had done, she would have had her thrown in a cell. Yet, the passports were stamped and everyone was wished a good day.

On the way back to the boat, they made the planned stop at the liquor store and procured the Port wine ordered by Pablo. Jack entered a sealed room and selected two exceptionally fine cigars which set him back seven hundred bucks. He had been assured by the proprietor that it would be practically a sin to smoke anything less with a fifty-year-old Tawny Port. While on the surface, the gift was a symbol of Jack's appreciation, he sensed it was also something deeper. When he was honest with himself, Jack knew that he was trying to earn Pablo's favor, which until recently, he didn't even know he wanted.

Jack would soon learn what Mariana knew well - Pablo had the ability to make people want his approval without saying a single word. He was vicious; but it was not his viciousness that had propelled him to the top. He was strategic, but that was not the catalyst for his success. He had family, but Pablo had seen family killed; he himself had even killed family for the family business. Pablo had charisma that was so strong, it affected all but the dead. That was the underlying current that fueled his ability to build an empire.

As they drove from the store to the docks, Mariana reflected on the first big assignment she was given by Pablo after her 18th birthday. Until that time, she had been an errand girl, a lookout, and a source of information. Now, he was ready to bring her deeper into his enterprise. Not only had she had earned his trust and respect, but he also thought of her as his own daughter.

There was a man that owed Pablo money. Doug "Wonderful" as he preferred to be called. Pablo hated him for many reasons, but Doug had been well-connected, so Pablo had left him alone until he learned that Doug had an unhealthy interest in teenage boys and girls. Pablo would not let this kind of behavior go unpunished on his streets. He took Mariana out for lunch one day and spoke to her about his plans.

"I have a special job for you my dear. There is a wicked man, who prefers the company of young men and women – do you know what I mean by this?"

"Yeah. Gross."

"Yes, very gross. I must stop this, and you can help me."

"Okay. What do you want me to do?"

"I want to use you as bait, to trap him in the act, and then he can be punished like the filthy pig that he is. Will you do this especially important thing for me?"

"Of course, Don Pablo."

A few days after her conversation with Pablo, Mariana stood on the corner near the café where Doug liked to have his coffee. She wore a very short skirt, and a thin T-shirt tied up in the front to expose her tight stomach. Her long, tan legs slid down into a pair of black pumps as she leaned provocatively against a bench. Periodically hiking her skirt a little, she would glance in his direction until she caught his eye. Then, she stared at him until he walked over and introduced himself.

"My name is Doug, people just call me Wonderful, what's your name, Baby?"

"You can just call me, Baby - I like that," Mariana said as she smiled at him and patted his arm.

"How old are you?"

"Old enough – sixteen is in the rearview mirror."

He smiled at her coy response.

"I've got a cool place around the corner; you wanna come up for some drinks, weed, and whatever?"

"Won't we get into trouble?"

"No, I've got you, Baby."

"Okay, let's go, Wonderful."

Diego and Pablo were seated in Doug's apartment when he arrived and entered with Mariana. He was instantly terrified but had no idea what was happening.

"Don Pablo, why are you here?"

"For many reasons, Douglas. First, you still owe me money."

"Yes, Don. I have a big score coming this week and I will pay you every cent. Cross my heart and hope to die."

"Hope to die?" said Diego. The normally quiet man had to laugh at the turn of phrase. "Hope is a powerful thing, Dougie. Be careful what you hope for."

Pablo laughed before an awkward silence overtook the room.

"Yes, I am concerned about the money, but I am more concerned with this?" Pablo said as he motioned to Mariana.

"Oh, this, ha! It's not what it looks like, Don! This is my niece, Leanna."

Pablo stood up, and walked toward Mariana, playing along with the ruse.

"What a pleasure to meet you, Leanna, was it?"

Mariana nodded, following Pablo's cues.

Pablo continued, "Leanna, you look a lot like a girl I know. Her name is Mariana. Which name would you prefer to be called by?"

Doug looked puzzled by the question.

"I prefer Mariana," she said politely.

"Mariana, why did this man bring you up here?"

"For beer and weed and probably sex if I had to guess by the pervy look in his eyes when he invited me up."

Pablo asked her, "And how old did he believe you to be?"

"I told him I was old enough but made a comment about sixteen."

Doug tried to mount a defense.

"Hey, wait a minute, none of that is true."

Pablo's fist hit the man in the face in the same manner that his own father had hit him years before.

"Don't lie to me, worm," Pablo said authoritatively.

"Don, no, it's not what you think."

The second blow came, knocking Doug back onto the couch as Pablo pulled out a gun.

"It is exactly what I think it is, you shit stain!" he screamed. "This is MY girl," he pounded his chest, "and we sent her here to prove once and for all that you are a disgusting pervert. You didn't think the rumors would make their way to my ears? You petulant fool!"

"I'm sorry, Don. It will never happen again. I swear it to you!" The man's tone conveyed his fear.

Pablo repeated Doug's words, "It will never happen again... This I know to be true, perhaps the truest statement your lying mouth has ever made."

Doug seemed to relax as he thought that the lesson was over and that he would live to see the sunset.

Then, Pablo took out the pistol his father had given to him and handed it to Mariana.

"Just like we practiced at the range. Aim at his balls."

Doug recoiled back into the couch as she raised the weapon and pulled the trigger. The explosion of the round was deafening in the small apartment.

Then the sound of Doug screaming filled the air before the shot had finished ringing out.

"Good job my dear. A little high – I think you hit his bladder because he has pissed himself," Pablo said in a matter-of-fact tone.

Diego found that to be hilarious and doubled over in laughter.

Mariana stood in silence, staring into the eyes of the man who had wanted to use her body to satisfy himself.

Pablo turned to Doug and said, "She's just learning, my apologies for having to shoot you again. My aim is better."

He placed the muzzle against the man's groin and as he started to struggle, Diego was instantly behind him holding his arms.

Pablo said, "You apparently don't understand the morals that govern our society. We aren't supposed to do those things with children." Then he pulled the trigger, and the man exploded in screams of pain far worse than before.

Pablo looked at Mariana and said, "This is a valuable lesson for you, do not break rules. Do not cross me."

He motioned Diego out of the way, raised the pistol and paused. For Doug and Mariana, the room seemed to freeze in time with the anticipation of what was to come next. For Pablo and Diego, this was like a movie they had watched many times, and almost seemed slightly bored with the spoiled ending.

Without another word, Pablo squeezed off a round into the man's head. Mariana watched it explode like it was in slow motion. The drapes behind the couch bore the full brunt of the man's brains, as the couch dutifully absorbed the flowing blood from the first two gunshots.

Then, Pablo raised the gun at Mariana and watched her terrified eyes fill with more fear.

"What did I just tell you, girl."

"Don't break the rules and don't cross you," she said as quickly as she could.

He smiled and lowered the gun, then tenderly, he said, "Yes, my dear, yes! It's a wonderful day to have an ice cream, don't you think."

Mariana, still dripping with fear, said as warmly as she could manage in a shaky voice, "Oh, yes, Don. That would be wonderful."

Pablo pushed his lips outward and nodded, glancing at Diego, who returned his nod of approval.

"A nice ice cream cone for the three of us, and then a stop at a tattoo parlor that owes me a favor. You are one of us now, and we will honor you with our mark." Pablo reached down and took Diego's left wrist, raising it to show her the mark.

She recalled feeling at the time that it was an honor. She had wanted Pablo's attention and approval, but as that scene in Doug's apartment had unfolded, she began to question her choices. Suddenly, Mariana felt trapped in a whirlpool she had not foreseen. She was now on a path of fear and fealty to Pablo, and she could see no escape.

The road came back into focus as her mind returned to the present. She looked down at her wrist and began feverishly rubbing the tattoo until she had rubbed through her own skin, and it began to bleed. It had taken her years to build up the courage to leave, and then a few more to convince herself to have the damn thing removed. She had never gone through with it, fearing that its removal would somehow unleash hell's wrath upon her.

It was the tattoo that she had planned to have removed in Fort Lauderdale - before she was reunited with the man that gave it to her. It was the same mark that Jack had noticed on Diego when they first met. It was the mark that Pablo would soon require Jack to take. The mark that meant complete and total fealty to the family of Don Pablo.

18

Windborne glided over the deep blue waters of the Gulf Stream. The southeast winds worked together with the current of the Stream to move them along at a quick clip. Jack had seen speeds as high as nine knots over ground, and he was pleased with their progress. This was a vastly different experience from the last time that he was in these waters, and his tension was beginning to subside. It took them just under fifteen hours to get well north of Middle Shoal in the Bahamas. Jack had timed it perfectly; the forecast northerly winds were building just after reaching their first waypoint. The northerlies would make for an easy, broad reach down the outside of the Bahamas, and his course would keep them twenty miles off the reefs. Jack had little appetite for risk.

The sun would come up soon, and Jack went below to log their position. Seated at the nav station, he looked up at Mariana, who was making soup in the galley.

"We're making good time," he said quietly since Diego and Pablo were still asleep in their berths. "We'll likely want to shorten sail as this northerly wind builds in."

She nodded in silence.

"Jack," she said and then paused. "Do you realize what's happening?"

"We're sailing a boat?" he asked in a mocking tone.

"Don't. I'm serious. This is serious shit."

"Ok, sorry. I thought I'd try to *not* be so serious for once."

"There's something on this boat. I don't know where, or what it is, but I know *that man,*" she nodded over her shoulder towards Pablo's room.

"She did seem to be riding a little low on the water line after we were provisioned and fully topped off all the tanks. I was going to say something but thought the yard had just missed the placement of the boot-stripe when they repainted her. Pablo looked me in the eye and promised that there were no drugs on board."

"He's a lot of things, but he isn't a liar," said Mariana as she was shaking her head. "If he said there's no drugs, there are no drugs."

They sat silently for a moment.

"What do you think it could be?" he asked innocently.

"His world revolves around four things: drugs, money, family, and punishment of offenders. We're pretty sure it's not drugs, definitely not family or punishment, so that leaves us with money."

"Do you have any idea of how much cash it would take to lower a boat this size in the water?"

She shook her head left to right.

"I think we'd be sitting on it, sleeping on it, and showering with it – if it was cash," he said.

Mariana's eyes opened wide, and she said, "Gold."

"What?"

"He's using your boat to move his gold. One of my assignments was to monitor the activity at his cash for gold stores. It's all part of his money laundering. That must be what the so-called watertight compartments are holding."

"You've got to be kidding me."

"Why do you act surprised? You rented yourself, me, and your boat to a sociopathic criminal."

"This is *my* fault again? You need to own your own shit kid."

Mariana said nothing. She turned her attention back toward the stove. Keeping her gaze fixed on the pot of soup, she said, "If there's gold, then there's guns to protect it. That I can promise you."

She had barely finished her sentence when Pablo's door opened, and he offered a sleepy hello.

"Where are we?" he asked.

Jack's answer stunned Mariana.

"What the fuck is on my boat Pablo, and I don't what to hear anymore bullshit."

Pablo walked over the nav station slowly and deliberately. He stared down at Jack, cocked his head to the right, and said, "What did I tell you about asking questions politely. Jack, I am not a man with the patience to repeat myself. Impoliteness makes me absolutely crazy, and when I get crazy, it makes me want to hurt people. You don't want me to hurt Mariana because you are insolent, do you?"

Jack looked up at the man, who despite his short stature, seemed to loom over him.

"I'm sorry, Pablo."

Pablo smiled, delighted by this change in Jack's attitude. He said, "Jack, humility is an important quality. Loyalty is more important. Do you really want to know what is on your boat?"

"Yes, I really want to know."

"Fine, we are at sea now, what's the harm in you knowing. But remember, my business is now your business, my friend. We are now in this venture together, and we will see it through to the end. ¿Comprende?"

Jack nodded solemnly.

Pablo motioned to the floorboards called *the cabin sole*, saying, "There is about twenty million dollars of gold under my feet," he said with a proud smile on his face. "Isn't that wonderful?"

Jack looked at Mariana. She had been dead-on in her guess. He now knew why *Windborne* had been sitting lower in the water.

"Any more questions, Captain?"

"What else?"

"You are a very invasive host!" said Pablo with humor, then added, "This is *my* charter."

"This is *my* boat." Jack said defiantly.

Pablo looked at Mariana as if she could explain why this man did not seem to understand that he was conversing with *The Don*.

"Let it go, Jack," she said.

"Listen to her, Jack. This is good advice she offers you."

As if he hadn't heard a word that Pablo had said, Jack stood up, and looked at him, saying, "I want to know everything that is on my boat that is not food, clothing, or personal care articles, and I want to know now."

Jack's volume was rising, and Diego had been awakened by the conversation. He poked his head out of his berth.

"Everything ok, Boss?"

Pablo smiled. "Yes, Jack and I are just talking about the items we are transporting."

The man nodded and disappeared back into the dark berth.

"Jack, I have been very patient with you, as Mariana can attest to. But I will continue to be patient with you only a little longer while you gain a better understanding of our relationship. I have always liked you Jack, and I would hate for our friendship to end. Especially over something so trivial."

"Then just tell me. Come on man, you and I know that you lured me into this - what did you call it - venture? You knew I was desperate, and you used it against me."

"That's what he does," uttered Mariana solemnly and softly. She couldn't believe that the words had come out of her mouth as she looked penitently toward Pablo. "I'm sorry Don, please forgive me."

"No, that's okay my dear. Get it off your chest. It's better that we are honest. What else would you like to tell our good captain about me? Please, carry on."

"No, really, I'm sorry."

"We all make mistakes, dear. I find that the key in life is not to make too many of them," he said as he smiled at her. Then, he looked at Jack and said, "Yes, Jack. I have other items. Paintings and other valuables – things which are important to me. You my friend, are going to help me move them to Colombia. I think it will take five trips, or five boats which you will oversee."

"What?" Jack asked in shock.

"Was I not clear about something?"

"Five trips? I didn't agree to that."

"Let me show you some interesting photos Jack."

Don Pablo went into his berth and came out with a handful of polaroid pictures. He dropped them on the nav station where Jack had been sitting. Jack picked them up and started going through them. His face looked perplexed at first, turning to shock, then fear. He saw pictures of the gold being sealed in. There were pictures of the artwork and valuables. Finally, he saw a picture of the guns.

When Jack finished, Pablo continued. "You see, Captain. You are illegally transporting gold, guns, and stolen artwork. Not to mention that you are helping someone being investigated by the feds leave the country with all of these items. I believe they call that aiding and abetting, yes? Copies of these pictures are with my team, and they have instructions to hand them over to the feds if you turn on me. If you want your license back, you will have it. But you will only have it if you do everything I ask of you. If not, you're nothing but a washed-up loser. And based on what my people told me in Norfolk, you'll spend the rest of your pathetic life on a barstool."

Jack could feel his fists clenching.

"Norfolk?"

"Yes, of course. Do you think I am such a fool as to call you out of the blue and hire you without checking up on you first?"

"I guess not," Jack said as he looked at the floorboards trying to picture the gold beneath them.

Pablo looked at Mariana with a slightly perturbed expression and bobbed his head to the left and right while saying, "He guesses not!" His tone was maniacal and sarcastic. "Well, Captain, you guessed well. No, I'm not a fool. Before I ever called you, I used my network to find you and have you watched. Then, and only then, after I was sure that you needed me more than I needed you, I called you 'out of the blue,'" he said making air quotes.

"So, you did take advantage of my desperation."

"I guess that's one way to look at it, Jack. I prefer to think that we are simply helping each other out. You clearly needed some guidance and focus, and I needed a boat from someone who needed money and wouldn't ask too many questions."

Jack looked pissed and Mariana could tell that he was winding up to respond; she saw his fists start to clench, along with his jaw. She was behind Pablo as he faced Jack, and Pablo could not see her. She shook her head rapidly trying to warn him off the deadly road he was walking on. Somehow, her pleading expression broke through his anger and adrenaline. Jack nodded to her, relaxed his hands, and sat back down.

"Ok, Jefe. Thanks for being honest with me. I feel better now," he lied.

"Bueno! I love it when plans come together, and we are friends who can enjoy a cruise! Tonight, after we dine, we will have some of that fine port and the cigars you bought – such a lovely gift, Jack!"

Pablo smiled at both of them as if they were children who had just been scolded. Now, the punishment was complete, and the nastiness was over. They were once again friends and family.

"Mariana, would you make me an espresso on the stove, please?"

"Yes, of course, Don."

"I will go out into the cockpit and wait for the sun to rise, bring my coffee up when it is ready."

Pablo smiled and climbed up the ladder, exiting the saloon and then sitting down in the cockpit. Once he was out of earshot, Mariana looked at Jack, and in a whisper, said, "Jack! Are you nuts? This guy kills people he doesn't like. For the love of God, please try to stay on his good side."

"I don't even know why I care. It's like part of me is acting like the guy I think I'm supposed to be, and part of me is saying, who gives a fuck? Maybe I'm playing this all wrong? What if this is my new career – running charters for the criminally insane. A drug runner, money runner, gun runner…"

"You're kidding right?"

"I don't know. I mean, really, who cares? Does any of it matter? Right, wrong, good, evil? It's all bullshit. I've played by the rules for too long, and this is my chance to break out of it. You're always talking about the universe and fate – maybe this is my fate."

"You don't know what you're talking about, Jack. It's not like playing cops and robbers, or pirates, or some other Hollywood bullshit. This guy will put a gun in your hand, tell you to point it at someone and pull the trigger. Is that what you want? You want to kill someone?"

"How do you know? Is that what he did to you?"

Tears welled up in her eyes as she said, "That's exactly what he did to me and then he did more. Then he used it against me to keep me close to him. He doesn't care about me, or you, or anyone, except himself and his psycho father."

"What happened?"

"I don't want to talk about it. At least not here, not now."

"Fair," he said in acknowledgment.

"I will tell you - when we're alone. I want you to understand. Hell, I need you to understand – for my sake and for yours. We've got to figure a way out of this together, and you need to knock off this outlaw pirate bullshit."

Jack said nothing in response to her as she turned back to the counter and started working on Pablo's espresso. He looked down at the pictures and thought about his fantasies of running a boat outside of the law. Now those fleeting thoughts were his new reality. *Did I manifest this?* He could feel himself slipping away into the darkness again and did nothing to stop it. Jack Kelly lacked the emotional reserves to fight anymore, and with his surrender, the once proud and dutiful captain took another long step in the wrong direction.

19

The chain of the eight cash-for-gold stores in Miami and Fort Lauderdale had been one of Pablo's most successful ventures, and his best money laundering scheme. First the drugs were sold by a dealer, who turned over the cash to a mule. The mule would take the cash to one of the gold stores and buy coins which were turned over to Pablo's security team. The business would deposit the cash into accounts and then invest in stocks, valuable art, collectibles, and real estate. It was all a shell game to throw off the government. At the current spot price on gold, his inventory of 400 troy ounce bars was worth about one-hundred million dollars with each bar valued at nearly eight-hundred thousand dollars. There were twenty-five bars worth twenty-million dollars, weighing a total of 675 pounds, sitting in double-glassed compartments in the bilge of *Windborne.* This was the first of the loads going south.

Pablo knew that the US government was incredibly good at tracking money. The end result of the 9/11 attacks was another move toward a police state, and decreased privacy was the new reality for anyone in America, especially the lawless. If the feds did seize his assets, that would include all of the real estate, brokerage, and bank accounts in the U.S., leaving him with damn little for his decades of work. The DEA, ATF, and Secret Service had been investigating him for years, but Pablo had well-paid people in these agencies, whose job it was to sound the alarm if things were getting too hot. That bell had been rung. The new president's administration was out to stop the evil drug kings, and Pablo was on their list. Now, it would be harder to do anything on a large scale because he was being watched carefully. The option of electronic transfers was out of the question, as was moving big piles of cash or gold through areas like shipping ports or airports which were heavily monitored. Now he was carefully moving chunks of his billion-dollar portfolio completely out of the U.S. government's reach.

Pablo sat back in the cockpit of *Windborne* and congratulated himself on his genius. He was tired of the United States anyway; he missed the freshness of the coffee, and the views of the mountains from the family ranch in Colombia. His father was getting old, and soon he would need to take over the global business operations. He had made his family a fortune, and worth far more than the money to him, he had made his father proud. It was now time to go home.

20

Sailing on the open ocean was intoxicating for Jack. It numbed him to all the cares on land. Yet he knew that offshore sailing was a freedom that could become an addiction. One in which the addict longs for the next fix - which lies about five hundred miles offshore. He had momentarily freed himself from the pain and reminders on terra firma, but new problems had emerged with Pablo and the cargo and were twisting him up inside. Now, the captain who sought to escape had nowhere left to run and hide.

The change in weather had brought squalls. Several cloud lines encircled them, bringing rain and fierce winds. While the guests filled the day with books, booze, and small talk, Jack sweated. He sweated inside the foul weather gear while he was drenched outside, keeping a firm grip on the helm. The series of squalls, each in its turn, took him further and further back in his mind, back to the massive storm in the Gulf Stream where he had lost Jen.

As Mariana started to step out on deck he shouted at her, “I’m serious, Mariana – don’t even think about coming up on deck without clipping in.”

“You’re ridiculous,” she said loudly as her long torso extended out of the companionway and into the cockpit.

“Think whatever you want to, as long as you do what you’re told.”

“So, it’s an order?”

“Damn straight. People that don’t follow my orders die.”

“Jack, these squalls aren’t that bad. We’ve barely seen ten-foot swells.”

“Look, have you ever been in this shit when it’s bad?”

“No.”

“Ok, well I have. And two people died. I have to live with that, and I don’t want any more weight added to what I already carry. Just clip in and stop fighting me.”

“Aye, Cap,” she said.

She reached down and grabbed the hook on the lanyard that lay at the base of the cabin hatch. After clipping in, she stepped out and slid down the seat towards him.

“How bad was it?” Mariana asked.

Jack stared off into the horizon and remained silent for nearly a minute after she had asked the question.

“It was bad at first, but manageable. *Windborne* is graceful - even in the nasty stuff. But there is one thing you just can't plan for… Any idea what that is?"

She thought for a few minutes before saying, "The weather is worse than the forecast?"

"Ok, two things you can't plan for. The other is a rogue wave."

"What's it like?"

"It's like someone hits you in the side of the head with a baseball bat when you are not looking."

"Tell me, Jack. I want to understand what happened to you."

He paused again, suddenly realizing that outside of the courtroom, he had never recounted the full story to anyone. He easily could have; it played in his mind like an endless loop, and he could never find the pause button. He wondered if telling her would help, or just make him relive the pain. Finally, after an awkward silence, he began.

"We'd been in it for a couple of days. It was getting worse, and we were beat to shit. By the time my watch ended, I'd been up for twenty hours and was completely exhausted. Our charter guest, Dave, was a super-experienced offshore sailor. I was comfortable leaving him on deck alone. Hell, he had more ocean experience than I did," Jack paused. The retelling of the night was adding weight to his soul with each spoken word. "We'd set up a watch rotation for him, Jen, and me. His girlfriend was puking buckets of pea soup, so we took her off the schedule. I was off duty and completely toasted. There was no longer a sense of duty, or obligation to my crew, I just wanted to sleep – it was all I could think about. When I finally got into my berth, I laid down next to Jen and fell fast asleep in seconds."

Jack paused and took a long, slow, deep breath, as if the gravity of what he was about to say would require more oxygen.

"All of a sudden, we were knocked down and rolled 360 degrees. The force, that sound…" Jack paused again as he relived the moment. "That sound still haunts me when it's quiet and I'm alone…" He sat quietly for a moment and looked out at the sea. "After *Windborne* was upright again, Jen went up to check on Dave… She forgot to harness up and clip in. By the time I got on deck – it couldn't have been two minutes later – she was gone." Jack looked intently into her eyes, "Now do you understand why I'm so damn adamant about you clipping in?"

Mariana sheepishly nodded while looking down to break his gaze. She felt guilty that her desire to know had made Jack relive something so painful.

"To say my life ended that day would be an understatement."

"I'm so sorry, Jack."

"Why do people always say they are sorry?"

It was a sincere question.

"I don't know, I guess it's 'cause we don't know what else to say."

"Yeah," he said in acknowledgement.

"How'd you cope?" she asked.

"I didn't – I ran into a bottle, then I morphed into *this."*

"This?"

"Yeah, whatever I am now. I'm not a captain or a criminal… yet. I don't know what I am or where I'm headed."

"You'll figure it out, Jack. You're a good man."

"I wish I shared your hope and faith."

He tried to force a smile.

"No more disagreements about clipping in, okay?"

"Roger that, Cap."

"Hey, you did the right thing by asking. I needed to share it with someone. Damn few know the whole story."

"Let me take the helm for a minute, Cap. You need a break. Worn out captains make bad decisions."

Jack nodded and slid out from behind the helm as she stood up to take it. He pointed down at the big compass to show her the heading, and without another word, he disappeared below.

Diego came out of his berth looking a little peaked. He made his way into the saloon and asked Jack, "Did you get everything settled with Jefe?"

"Yeah, no worries, mate," Jack replied dryly.

Diego nodded in approval. Part of his role was to ensure that there was harmony and order in Pablo's universe. If harmony wasn't possible, he would kill the people that didn't understand their place in the order. He had concerns as it related to Jack, because, since they were at sea, he couldn't just kill him. They needed Jack, and Diego was unaccustomed to this feeling.

Jack asked, "Coffee?" as he started to prepare his own brew.

"Yes, please. I feel like I've been in the sleep of the dead."

"It's normal, Diego," Jack said. "When people get offshore and finally relax, they usually sleep very deeply. For you, I'd guess that you're relaxing because you don't have to look over your shoulder every thirty-seconds."

Jack's comment gave Diego pause. He wasn't sure if it was an innocent observation or a dig. He decided it was the former, and that Jack was right.

"Huh, I never thought about it like that. You're right. I mean, it's not like you're going to put one between my eyes, eh, Captain Jack?"

Jack smiled, softly laughed, and then said, "No, I signed a charter captain's pledge not to shoot my guests."

Diego laughed at Jack's dry joke and sat down while Jack returned to the chart table and began updating the logs. After the coffee was ready, he poured two cups and joined Diego at the table. They drank in silence as Diego glanced at pictures of white sandy beaches in a cruising magazine that Jack had on the rack.

"Can we do this?" he asked innocently.

"I don't see why not," Jack answered with a smile.

A few minutes later, Jack said, "I'm going up on deck to take a look at the squall lines."

Diego nodded as Jack put on his foul weather gear, slid into his combination inflatable flotation device and storm harness, and pulled a lanyard made of nylon webbing off the wall. He clipped one end to the harness and then looked at Diego.

"Diego, I know you guys don't like it when I tell you what to do, but I must insist that we all wear harnesses if we go on deck in a storm, and never without me or Mariana, okay? You saw my boat when it came into the yard, right?"

Diego nodded.

"Well, that's what can happen in a storm. It rolled, Diego. Two people died. I don't want any more dead passengers, so clip in like this," Jack demonstrated the motion, "then, you take this end and clip it into one of the U-shaped steel tie-in points on deck. The first time you go out, let one of us walk you through it."

"Sure thing, Jack."

"And Diego, do me a favor, if Jefe pushes back, I'm counting on you to help me convince him. I mean, it's your job to protect him, yeah?"

"That it is, Jack. I'll make sure he does it."

Jack turned and climbed up the ladder onto the deck, clipping in before he stepped completely out.

He loudly said to Mariana, "Thanks for the break. I'm good, you head on down and get some rest."

"Okay, Cap."

Mariana handed him the helm, and noted with her index finger that they were still on course.

"Well done!" He said enthusiastically.

"Yeah, well, I've got a good teacher," she complimented him as she unclipped and stepped down the ladder, once again bumping her head and completing her positive ritual. Jack laughed as he watched it unfold.

Despite what Jack might say to her about making her own decisions, he was deeply disturbed by the fact that she was right back in the fire she had tried to outrun. He was unconcerned that the flames from that same fire were beginning to feel like warmth to his own soul. For the next half an hour, his mind drifted between Mariana, Jen, the helm, and the compass. Lost in his mind as he often was these days, he hadn't noticed how much the sky had changed until a sudden bright burst of light startled him, and he felt the soundwave as it roared through the sky.

"Son of a bitch – lightning storm."

The approaching clouds seemed to crouch on the horizon, appearing to touch the sea itself. Jack stared at them with anger and defiance, as if he were a medieval knight ready to fight a dragon with a broadsword.

He knew that he needed to brief the crew quickly, so he switched on the autopilot and went below. As he dropped into the cabin, he saw that Pablo was at the table with Diego having coffee and talking, while Mariana worked tirelessly in the galley preparing them more coffee and food. Her nap had never materialized.

She looked up at him as he climbed down and asked, "How's it looking out there, Cap? Was that thunder I just heard?"

"Yes, it was. It looks like a shit-storm sandwich - hope you're hungry," he said, managing a wry smile. "I need to brief you guys, can you put that on hold for a few minutes?"

"Sure thing," she said without emotion.

She wondered, *Was it chance or fate that brought me back into Pablo's storm? I don't think I can…*

"Mariana! Hey, do you mind joining us? Mentally and physically?"

"Yeah, uh, sorry, Jack. I… I got lost in my thoughts for a minute."

"No worries, grab yourself a cup of coffee and sit down here," he said as he patted the seat next to him.

As Mariana poured her coffee, she could hear the conversation behind her but none of it registered. She was still fighting to get back to the present. When she sat down, Pablo offered her a warm, fatherly smile. He could sense her distress. He also knew that the cause of her upset was not the storm outside.

Jack began his briefing by holding up a laminated piece of paper with a stain on the corner, the last time it had been used was by Jen in the Gulf Stream. He began to give them a sobering overview of the situation they faced.

“We’ve got an electrical storm heading our way. So, first things first, give me all of your electronics - phone, tablets, computers, anything you care about. We’ll wrap them in aluminum foil and put them in the microwave - it will act as a Faraday cage.”

“A whataday cage?” Diego asked.

“Faraday cage. It’s an enclosure that keeps electromagnetic fields out. If the boat gets hit by lightning, it can demolish electronics - comms, nav, etcetera.”

The group nodded in silence and Pablo asked the next question, “Isn’t it like a million to one that we’d get hit by lightning?”

Before Jack could answer, Mariana broke in, “Actually, it’s only 1 in 1,000 – not great odds.”

The group stared at her in surprise.

“What?” she asked. “Why are you all looking at me like that?”

It lightened the mood momentarily and Jack said, “Oh, no reason Dr. Science, I guess I missed the section titled *Knowledge of Obscure Facts* on your sailing resume.”

Everyone, including Mariana, laughed at his retort. She tossed a crumpled napkin at him playfully. Jack smiled at her and winked. Pablo noticed the exchange and wondered if something was developing between them and was conflicted. Part of him hoped that it would, but a larger part of him hoped that it wouldn't. She was like a daughter to him, and Jack was a man he admired.

Diego asked, "But aren't we safe out here? I thought lightning struck trees." And then, in a western drawl, he said, "I don't see no trees out'n here greenhorn."

Jack's smile formed slowly, as the others laughed. He looked at Diego smiling, and for the first time since he met him, Jack saw him as human.

"That's pretty good, Diego," said Jack. "Yeah, there are no trees, but there's a fifty-foot aluminum mast that's pretty attractive to lightning. In fact, you're sitting right next to it."

Diego shifted uncomfortably as he looked at the thick aluminum mast base that ran through the cabin and down onto the keel of the boat. Up until that moment, it had been just something he had to walk around to get into his cabin. Now, he saw it as an ominous threat and slid a few inches away from it.

Jack continued, "There's also coaxial cable for all of the electronics inside it. All right, back to the really fun stuff here. The first and most important rule - and I cannot emphasize this enough - is that everyone needs to follow my orders promptly and without question." Jack paused and looked at Pablo, who stared uncomfortably back at him.

"Pablo, I know you are not a man accustomed to taking orders. I need you to trust me here, okay?"

"Yes, Jack. I understand that the situation has changed."

"Good. The second rule, is that you and Diego are to remain below decks unless I give you permission to go above."

Pablo looked uncomfortable at the suggestion that he had to have Jack's permission to do *anything,* but he remained silent.

"The third rule, is that no one, not me, not Mariana, not either of you, go above deck without clipping in. Got it?"

Jack then showed them his harness and explained how the system worked, and why it was necessary. By this point, the egos had been quelled due to a new understanding of Mother Nature's sheer fury.

As Jack finished the briefing, he could see acceptance and resolve in their eyes and knew that his message and tone had done the important work of humbling the proud men. He took no pleasure in his accomplishment, he felt only the burden of three more souls that were his to save or lose. Despite his lack of control, he felt a deep sense of ownership. Jack Kelly was a man that worked better when he was focused – something he had not felt since they abandoned the search for Jen in the Stream.

The Captain wrapped it up, "We've got an hour or two before it's on top of us, so make your confessions and say your prayers if you're into that sort of thing. If there are no questions, that's it for now. Gather up your devices and give them to Mariana. She'll give you your PFD. Keep it near you. We'll tell you if you need to put it on."

He turned to Mariana and said, "First watch is mine."

Jack stood up and walked to the ladder. Then, he looked up at the closed hatch, and then back at them before he began slowly climbing up. His face wore a look of experience and sheer resolve that none of them had seen before. Licensed or not, the man going on deck was the Captain.

21

An hour after the briefing, Jack stood on deck, dripping wet in his foul weather gear. The seas had built to twenty feet, and Jack was thankful that the shoals of the Bahamas were now well behind them. *Windborne* was running south with the storm. The captain had learned well enough that fighting storms at sea was a fool's errand – he did not need to be taught this lesson a second time.

The gusts of wind sent the rain into the exposed sections of his skin like a thousand tiny needles stinging him and reminding him of nature's fury. Fortunately, his eyes were covered with ski goggles - a trick he had learned from his friend, Simon, an ocean crossing sailor of some renown.

The lightning was no longer on the distant horizon, it was now uncomfortably close and becoming more frequent. Jack called down and let Mariana and the others know what was going on, then he returned to his vigilant watching of the storm, as if by staring at it hard enough he could push it away with the sheer force of his own will. It wasn't hope, fear, or optimism that drove his intensity in this moment; it was pure desperation. The thought that he might have to pick up the radio handset and call another mayday brought the realization that death would be preferable. The dance went on.

Then suddenly, *crack!* Lightning hit the mast and mercifully didn't hit Jack, despite him being wet and charged. He looked down at his rubber boots and wondered if they saved him, or if the gods had let him live because they weren't done punishing him.

The damage assessment began immediately as the boat veered off course. *Damn, lost the autopilot.*

"Son of a bitch," Jack muttered as he grabbed the helm. He began to heave-to, bringing *Windborne* alongside the wind, with the helm and headsail countering each other as the boat sat, parked in the heavy seas. Then, Jack unclipped and moved across the cockpit, sliding out the strong oak storm hatch boards from the entryway. Once it was open, he looked down into a dark cabin and yelled to Mariana, "Report!"

"We're taking on water!" Mariana yelled back.

"Get your lifejackets on and see if you can find out where the water is coming from." Jack shouted.

"Got it!" She yelled back.

"Mariana – how much water?"

"It's coming in fast!"

Jack secured the hatch and went to the holding area for one of the life rafts and with the boost of adrenaline, easily lifted the 110-pound inflatable raft out of its cradle and removed its lashings. He secured the painter line to an aft cleat, being careful to run it under the lifelines, and heaved it into the water on the leeward side of the boat. Quickly, he pulled the painter line hand over hand taking up the slack and then gave it a hard jerk to activate the gas cylinder. The boat inflated quickly and drifted off downwind until the painter line was taut. Reluctantly, Jack picked up the radio to call a mayday, but it was dead. The lightning had knocked out the electronics.

"Shit! Shit! Shit!" He yelled in frustration. Next, he grabbed the new storm anchor out of the locker. *Here we go again, maybe I should just let you sink, girl, You seem to be destined for the bottom of the sea*. Jack stopped and seriously thought about the benefits of letting the boat sink. No more gold to deliver, no more Pablo.

He clipped into the jackline that ran the length of each side of the sailboat, and with great effort in the heavy seas, worked his way forward. Once on the bow, he secured the sea anchor to the sturdy cleats used for the boat's anchor line and tossed it under the bow pulpit into a raging sea. Then, he scrambled back to the cockpit and released the sheets controlling the sails as the boat went into irons. The sails flapped noisily and aimlessly, as *Windborne's* bow rounded up into the wind and began to quickly drift back on the sea anchor. Fortunately, the large waves had gentle slopes, so there was little risk of the boat rolling. Once the pressure was off the sails, he furled the headsail, and then dropped the mainsail into the stack pack. As soon as Jack felt *Windborne* tug on the sea anchor, he went down below as quickly as possible.

Upon entering the cabin, he saw them scrambling to find the leak. Emergency lanterns and flashlights produced eerie illumination in the dark cabin.

Jack yelled, “Where’s it coming from?”

“I think it’s behind this cabinet,” Diego yelled back.

Jack headed over while barking orders, “Mariana, get the ditch bag ready. Take our electronics out of the microwave and put them into the bag. Get the sat phone and EPIRB too.”

The emergency positioning-indicating radio beacon would be picked up by the Cospas-Sarsat satellites so that rescuers would know where they were.

“Aye, Cap.”

“Then, get up on deck and start working the manual bilge pump. If we can’t find this leak and plug it, we are going to get wet. The life raft is already deployed leeward aft.”

“Roger,” was all she said as she harnessed up, clipped in, and climbed out on deck.

Jack began searching for the leak with the men. He was rapidly emptying lockers and cabinets, tossing things out of their way as if it were discarded garbage. None of it mattered now.

“Jack!” Pablo shouted loudly. “Don’t you let this boat sink with my gold you son of a whore! I will kill you!”

Jack paused, stunned by the man’s words. He quickly turned and looked antagonistically at Pablo.

"Are you kidding me, dude. Fuck you and fuck your gold! I'll kill you myself if you utter one more fucking word!"

Upon Jack's outburst, Diego stopped looking for the leak and turned to face Jack. He wouldn't let this captain disrespect his boss; the insult could not stand unchecked. Now, the two men stood eye to eye while the water continued to flood into the cabin.

"Get the fuck out of my way, Diego," Jack said with intensity. "Are you two really this fucking insane? This boat is sinking fast, and it'll be on the sea floor in minutes unless we stop this water!"

Diego stood still, unmoved by Jack's words. He could feel the water rising around his ankles. The automatic bilge pump, along with the other electronics had failed. Mariana's feverish work on the manual pump was futile - she was losing the battle with the sea.

Without thought, Jack head-butted Diego so hard that it almost knocked him out. The strong man stumbled backward, and Jack grabbed him by the throat with his left hand and began pummeling his face with his right hand. Despite his decades of martial arts training, there was no form, only function. That function was one of a jackhammer on Diego's face. Suddenly, Diego was the source of all Jack's pain - past, present, and future. *Diego* was now the storm that Jack wanted to end, and he would have his vengeance. His action was so powerful and decisive that Diego never had a chance to defend himself.

"Jack! Stop it!" Pablo shouted.

Jack ignored him and just kept beating the man as his facial bones began to collapse.

Mariana, who had heard Pablo screaming, stuck her head inside the cabin and saw Pablo pulling a semi-automatic pistol from under his shirt.

"Pablo, no!" she yelled. "Jack, stop, stop!"

Mariana's words broke through the rage. He dropped Diego, looked down at him and said slowly, "Oh god, what have I done?" Then, he looked at Pablo, who held the gun in his hand, and asked, "I suppose you're going to shoot me now?"

Pablo, with tremendous effort in the heavy seas, pulled himself to his feet and turned toward Jack, who was now standing in nearly knee-deep water.

Mariana screamed, "Pablo, no, please don't!"

Pablo faced her and said, "It's ok, child." Then, he turned and raised the gun towards Jack before saying, "Step away."

With a puzzled look on his face, Jack moved out of the way, Pablo placed the gun on Diego's forehead and squeezed the trigger.

"What the fuck, Pablo!" Jack shouted.

Mariana glared at Pablo sullenly.

"Jack! Shut up and focus. Save this goddamn boat and my gold or I'll shoot you next!"

Jack pulled Diego out of the way and dropped him in the water, which began to turn red with his blood. Mariana silently and dutifully returned to deck without a word and went back to her job hand-pumping the bilge. Alive or dead, she knew that her life was over.

Jack yanked open a cabinet and pulled out a battery-operated reciprocating saw, which he kept on board for exactly this type of emergency. Without regard for aesthetics, he began ripping away at the seating and cabinetry to find the leak. Within a minute, he had exposed an area that revealed the hole.

The lightning had shot down the mast through a loose grounding cable that the yard installed incorrectly and lay on the side of the hull. From there, it went right through the hull – just inches below the waterline.

"I found the leak!" Jack shouted as he turned to rummage through another cabinet. He pulled out an orange bag marked, *EMERGENCY*. Then, he poured the contents of the bag on the table and found a two-part epoxy clay that would set-up under water, along with a bung plug. He tore open the package of epoxy and molded it until it was solid grey, then he took the tapered cylindrical plug and molded the clay around it. He kept a shot filled dead-blow hammer in the kit, and he used it to pound the bung plug into the hole until it was wedged in tightly. Once the water had stopped rushing in, he took his thumb and pushed the epoxy down around the plug and hull.

Pablo watched with curiosity in complete silence. There was no fear in his eyes, only concern. He couldn't imagine facing his father to explain that he had lost twenty-million dollars of the family's gold. Now that the water was no longer rushing into the boat, a smile began to form on his face as he watched Jack work to seal the leak. His reputation with his father would remain intact, and Jack Kelly had proved himself to be the right man for the job. Once again, Pablo thought about how proud his father would be when he could see the brilliance of his plan and choice of players.

Jack wiped off the area around the plug.

"Once the water drops, I'll build up some glass around it – that should hold until Puerto Rico. We'll have to spend a few days in a yard. Do you know anyone in San Juan?"

"Yes, of course, Jack. It's no problem. It's good that we can make it to Puerto Rico. We won't have to clear customs since it's U.S. territory."

"Yeah, but we'll be back under their long reach," Jack said defeatedly as he gathered up the items on the table and placed them back in the emergency kit.

Why the fuck did you kill him, Pablo?" Jack asked as he looked down at Diego.

"He was stealing from me. I found two of my gold bars in his bag."

"Really?"

"Why are you surprised, are you really that pure of a man? Gold drives men to do things they wouldn't otherwise do – I should know."

"He seemed so loyal."

"In the end, men are loyal only to themselves."

Jack stared at Pablo and let the words sink in. His own garden of cynicism was flourishing like a rich bed of coral and Pablo's words were nutrients.

"I've known for some time, and I was going to kill him in Colombia. It doesn't matter, he was half dead after your beating," he smiled at Jack with approval.

Jack shook his head in disgust.

"Diego was a very, very vain man. He would not have liked his face after what you did to it." Pablo laughed at his observation. "So fierce, like an animal!" Pablo's last words revealed a tone of approval, but there was something else about the way he said it that Jack couldn't put his finger on. It was something more than admiration.

Jack said, "We should give him a proper burial at sea."

"Yes, of course Jack. Tell me how I can help with this, it is the least I can do. And I will take care of his mother financially, she will have nothing to worry about for the rest of her life. Of course, his death will be hard on her. He was her only son, and she did love him dearly," Pablo said in a rare moment of concern for someone other than himself or his father.

Jack began to pull the dead man up under his arms and toward the ladder. He asked Pablo, "Were you two friends?"

"Friendly yes, friends no. Learn this from me, Jack. There is no such thing as friends. There are people that need or want something from you; you may think they are your friends but find out how much they care about you once you have nothing left that they want."

"Is it lonely?"

"Why do you ask me? You already know the answer to that question, *Captain*."

Jack nodded in agreement. He did know.

"He was an employee, nothing more. Diego was loyal. I value that above all - remember that. But he was also impetuous and at times, ill tempered – a hothead. He is dead because he underestimated you and because he hesitated. Those are not qualities well-suited for my business. If he had understood who you are and what drives you, he would have moved on you first, and it probably would have been an even match. A different outcome, perhaps? We might all be sharing a cold beer now."

"Who am I and what drives me?" Jack asked desperately.

"I could tell you, Jack, but I won't. It is better that you discover this for yourself."

22

After the clearing winds had blown through and the last of the storm-driven waves had spent their energy, an eerie calm descended on the sea, the boat, and Jack. He felt nothing inside. The joy and passion he had once felt as a captain was gone. A gray mist enshrouded the horizon that painted a complete picture of Jack's soul - wandering aimlessly, changing its shape, and dimming the light.

Diego's lifeless body lay on the port cockpit seat in the stiffness of death, wrapped in an old canvas tarp, tied tightly, and weighted down with a spare dinghy anchor. They had made a group decision to hold the burial at sunrise and Jack couldn't wait to get the body off of his boat. *His boat* – he almost laughed aloud when he thought of *Windborne* being his; he knew deep inside that he had sold his boat and soul to Pablo. Desperation had driven him and Pablo had leveraged it. He was tired of dissecting his choices and morals. *Fuck it,* he thought.

Jack couldn't stop glancing over at the corpse.

"I guess I'm the one that killed you in a manner of speaking, Diego. That makes three - if you were wondering – you weren't my first. You were the first person I killed that I hated, but it didn't feel as good as I imagined it would. But I guess you know all that, huh buddy? How many people did you send on to the next life?"

He stopped for a minute and looked out at the mist.

"Well, if nothing else, I understand that your boss hasn't an ounce of loyalty to anyone. Not to you, not to Mariana, and certainly not me. I don't see how I'm getting out of this one alive... Save a seat for me at the table in hell."

Jack's thoughts drifted aimlessly in his new pirate state of mind. At first it had been a joke, and now it was his new reality. He was a defrocked captain smuggling gold, and now, an accessory to murder. *Mom would be so proud,* he thought sarcastically.

Next to him sat an open bottle of rum and a tin cup from *Pusser's* in the British Virgin Islands. The cup held memories of Jen while the rum blocked them out. *She would not be happy with me at all.* But it was merely an observation; her approval was less of a burden on his conscience. He wondered why it didn't bother him more. *Did I stop loving her or is my heart just that hard now? I'm wasting my time with all of this useless introspection.*

"Hey." He heard Mariana say.

He felt as if he was being recalled from a dream.

"Hey, back at ya."

"A little early for rum, Boss... Don't ya think?"

"I've been thinking too much, and this seems to help with that. You look like you could use some too."

She sat down next to him, and he handed her the cup. She looked at the Royal Navy rum terminology on the back of the cup. It listed the instructions as to the size of an appropriate sip from another sailor's cup. She zeroed in on *"Gulpers: One, but only one, big swallow from another's tot."*

"Gulpers." She said aloud. Then she hoisted the cup first to Jack, then to Diego's body, before taking a long swallow.

"Looks like we'll make a good sailor out of you yet," Jack said as he managed a tired smile.

He watched Mariana as she looked out into the distant horizon. He was finding himself increasingly attracted to her and was fighting it off with what little strength he had left.

"Sun's coming up," said Jack. "Let's get our friend here off the boat. Go down and let Pablo know that it's time."

Mariana disappeared below and left Jack alone once again with his thoughts and the rum. He thought about Laura, and wondered if he should just ditch the boat in Puerto Rico and take the first flight back to Virginia. *There was a connection, I think we would make a nice couple. A normal life, a loving wife, and a sweet daughter. What would it feel like to wake up every day in that world?* Then he looked out at the sun coming up over the still water as it burned through the mist and knew that this was his home regardless of whatever good and bad went along with it. He knew that he would be restless and miserable if he returned to a life on shore, and that misery would bleed onto every life around him, corrupting all of them.

Pablo appeared with Mariana. He was dressed in fine linen trousers, a Havana style short-sleeve button up shirt, huarache sandals, and gold rimmed aviator sunglasses. Mariana, in contrast, looked like a sailor at sea. She wore the same dirty t-shirt that she'd had on for two days, stained with grease, port wine, and Diego's blood. Tight jean shorts displayed her fit body, and her hair was pulled back to reveal the shaved side of her head.

"Good morning, Captain."

"Buenos Dias, Pablo."

Pablo smiled broadly hearing the Captain's greeting in Spanish. "Maravilloso, Jack! I hope you don't mind; I've prepared some words for the burial – would you like me to begin now, Capitan?"

Jack was surprised at his deference.

"Uh, yeah. Sure thing, Pablo."

Pablo bowed his head solemnly and began.

"Diego is gone now from this earthly dwelling and has left behind those who mourn his absence. Grant that we may hold his memory dear, never bitter for what we have lost, nor in regret for the past, but always in hope of the eternal Kingdom, where you will bring us together again. Through

Christ our Lord." After he finished, he made the sign of the cross. Out of respect, Jack and Mariana joined him in the ritual.

Jack had been to a few Catholic funerals as a kid and recognized the prayer. For a brief moment, through the fog of his exhaustion and fatigue, he tried to reconcile the mournful religious expression from the man who had pulled the trigger. A flood of conflict overloaded his mind, and he started to cry. They weren't tears of mourning for Diego. They were tears of sadness originating from the gash that was widening in his soul and separating him from all that he had once loved and held dear.

"Diego, you were many times at my side, and you did my bidding." Then, he looked at Mariana. "This must be a hard day for you, he was there when we brought you into our world, remember?"

Tears began to roll down her face for a different reason. She nodded as she wiped her eyes with the back of her hands.

Pablo continued, "Look at the three of us, a small family grieving for a departed loved one. This is a moment we will all remember."

Pablo paused like a preacher about to deliver the altar call, then in a building crescendo, he said, "Diego's death was avoidable. He stole from me! He was disloyal to me! I picked this man up from the slums and I paid him generously! If he or his mother ever needed ANYTHING..." Pablo stopped his rant and took a deep breath, regaining his composure.

"Jack, Mariana, position the body to be sent over the side."

With great effort, Jack and Mariana lifted the tarp and positioned it outside of the cockpit coaming and at the edge of the boat. When they were finished, they looked up at Pablo.

"Do either of you have any words before we send him to his grave?"

Mariana spoke first, "Diego, you watched over me in my teen years, and kept me on a path. It wasn't the right path…" She glanced at Pablo to see if she had said the wrong thing, but his eyes were hidden behind dark grey lenses. She continued nervously, "You did what you thought was right. I guess that's all we can do sometimes."

Jack began, "Diego, I've gotta admit, I didn't really like you at first. If I'm honest, I hated you. But after a while, you started to grow on me. I think in another life, we could have been friends. Don't forget to save that seat at the table for me."

Pablo continued, "Diego, in the end, I found you to be a lying, cheating, bastard. Despite this, I didn't torture you, and I will take care of your mother. This is why I will always be better than you, Diego. You are fortunate that I am such a caring man, or your mother would be trapped in poverty without you to provide for her. You always lacked the ability to look into the future, Diego." He paused for a few moments of silence and then said with authority, "Send him down."

Jack and Mariana pushed the tarp holding Diego over the edge of the boat and into the dark water. The weighted down canvas tarp hit the water feet first and made a clean entry with only a small splash. Fast, finite, and final. Diego disappeared quickly from their view, but slowly from their thoughts.

23

The day they sent Diego to the depths was morally, mentally, and physically exhausting. Within minutes of the tarp disappearing below the surface and with another full glass of rum in hand, Jack began the repairs to his once again storm-battered sailboat.

"Mariana," Jack called out. "Do you know how to install a bilge pump?"

"I do, Jack."

"There's a spare in the forward sail locker, and the electrical kit is with the tools. Don't forget to put the shrink wrap tubing on *before* you connect the wires. I always forget the part."

Mariana nodded and turned away quickly to get to work. She wasn't in any mood for conversation – none of them were. Her head was pounding from the lack of sleep, and she knew there wasn't likely to be a nap on today's schedule.

The boat was a mess, but Jack had learned his lesson well in the Gulfstream and had purchased spares for all major repairs. The lightning had knocked out all the electronics, fried the alternator, auto-pilot, and bilge pump. By the end of the day, those important systems would be back online.

"Pablo, I could use a hand today if you're up for it."

Pablo's face seemed to light up upon hearing Jack's request. "Yes, of course, my friend. Of course."

"Great, now that we have a calm, I want to go over the side and mold in some underwater epoxy around the plug from the outside. I'd like you on deck in case I need support."

"Yes, I'm happy to help you, Jack."

"Okay, you might want to put something on that you don't mind getting dirty."

"All right, I'll be back up in a moment."

While Pablo went below to change, Jack pulled off his t-shirt and located the small tube of epoxy putty in his tool bag, along with a well-used piece of wet-or-dry sandpaper. He dug around in the locker and pulled out a spare line that he would use to tether himself to the boat. He shoved the epoxy and sandpaper into the side pocket of his swimsuit and secured the line to the amidships cleat which was the nearest to the hole in the boat. In the gear locker, there were floaties and snorkeling gear for guests; he lifted the lid, rummaged around, and pulled out a mask. Then, he dropped the swim ladder over the side before tying the line around his midsection and securing it with a bowline knot. By the time he'd finished, Pablo was topside again.

"All set, Captain."

Jack looked at Pablo quizzically, he was surprised that the man had called him Captain. He desperately wanted to dwell on that to understand the reason, but his exhaustion and the task at hand shoved the thought out of his mind.

"Great. I'm going to slide in here and take a look, I may need you to hand something down to me."

"Why the line?"

"Things have a way of happening out here, as you may have now realized."

Pablo nodded with understanding as he watched Jack climb down the ladder and into the very deep water. He noticed Jack's muscle tone, admiring his firm arms.

Jack thought that the water looked dark and ominous, knowing it held secrets, predators, and the dead. He pulled the mask down over his face and ducked under the surface, working his way up the side of the boat. He was glad that she sat still in the calm seas. When he reached the hole, he gently pushed on the bung plug and could feel that it was secure. Then he swam back to the ladder and pulled himself up a rung until his upper body was out of the water. He swung his arm through the ladder to hold himself up. With the other hand, he reached down and fished the tube of epoxy putty out of his pocket and held it up to Pablo.

"Okay, take this and tear off a piece about a finger length long. Then mold it together until it's all one color. Once the color is uniform, form it into a long worm – six to eight inches long."

"Yes, I saw you do this last night."

Pablo took the container and began molding the epoxy while Jack hung off the side of the boat. Jack started thinking about the "Captain" he received from a man who was deferent to no one. *Was it because I caved in Diego's face? Does he respect me now?*

Jack quickly realized that everything Pablo did was calculated and served *his* purposes. Breathing in deeply, the captain closed his eyes and exhaled while he contemplated the stack of decisions that landed him in this spot. The late season charter he accepted. *Greed*. Leaving the Bahamas and trying to beat the storm's arrival in the Gulf Stream. *Arrogance*. Taking the job with Pablo. *Desperation*. He wanted to make his next decision a good one, but his own compass was damaged. He, like *Windborne,* was drifting in the current.

"Okay, here you go, Jack."

Pablo handed him the piece of putty. Jack took it from him and pushed off from the boat, swimming down to the hole.

"Take up the slack on my line and give me a little support to hold me above the water."

Pablo reached down and took the line, pulling in the slack until he had a little tension on it.

"Good."

Jack took the sandpaper and scuffed up the epoxy paint; then, he carefully wrapped the epoxy worm around the bung plug and flattened it between the wood plug and the hull. When he was satisfied with the repair, he kicked back away from the boat and looked up into the sky, floating lifeless for a few moments.

Pablo examined the man carefully. He had chosen him for a purpose, and now it seemed that Jack was almost all the way into his fold. Pablo never missed an opportunity to take advantage of desperation - he found it to be a great motivator, second perhaps only to fear and love. *Jack will take a little more molding, but he has all of the right qualities for my needs. And then of course, there are the other reasons… I wonder what Captain Jack Kelly would think if I told him all of it? Then of course, there is my father, too…* Pablo looked down at the man floating in the water as he continued to let his own mind drift.

After a few minutes, Jack turned over, ducked back under the water, and swam back toward the hole. He felt the putty and it was solid. The bond to the hull was better than he had hoped. *Got to love epoxy putty.*

Jack popped his head out of the water, pulled up the mask, and called up to Pablo, "Looks good."

"Bueno."

Jack swam back to the ladder, pulled himself on deck and slid the line out from around his waist.

"Mind giving me a hand with the alternator?"

"Not at all! I used to work on the tractors on our property with my father. I know my way around a diesel engine."

"You are nothin' if not full of surprises, Pablo." Jack laughed as he shook his head.

During the morning, it almost felt congenial with Pablo, but as the day wore on, his true nature would reveal itself in little flashes of impatience. Tightened lips, a furrowed brow, and the small sighs. Jack could feel himself being pulled toward Pablo in a swift rip-current, but he didn't know which direction to swim to find his way to shore. He could feel himself giving up and going along with it, and he was starting to feel that this was perhaps the best course for everyone.

24

Jack felt his heart begin to race as soon as the island of Puerto Rico came into view. Even though they wouldn't need to clear into customs, the possibility still existed that they would be boarded. He knew that no amount of denying his knowledge of the cargo would save him from the United States Code - the laws which he was most flagrantly violating. It was his vessel, and he would be held responsible. He started singing a sea shanty to soothe his frayed nerves.

Oh, me name was Captain Kidd
As I sailed, as I sailed
Oh, me name was Captain Kidd
As I sailed
Oh, me name was Captain Kidd
God's laws I did forbid
And most wickedly I did
As I sailed, as I sailed

Jack set a waypoint on the new auto pilot he had installed after the lightning strike and ducked down below. He asked Pablo and Mariana to sit down with him for a briefing. As they arrived at the saloon table, they saw his tablet showing the Port of San Juan in some detail. They slid into the seats and waited for Jack to begin.

"Mariana, let's bring you up to speed first. Pablo called some of his people on the sat phone and he's arranged for us to go into a yard in San Juan."

Mariana nodded silently as she took in the information. Jack examined her and thought that she looked exhausted and hopeless, like a war refugee wandering along, hoping to find respite somewhere.

"Pablo, I think in order to lessen the attention on us, it might be a good idea if we dropped you in a marina, or a 'dock and dine' and then met up with you later. Me and Mariana can pass for the average cruising couple – you add a different and out of the ordinary dimension to that look. Plus, you didn't clear out with us, so that's another good reason for you to keep a low profile."

"Yes, Jack. This makes good sense."

Pablo seemed pleased that Jack had cleverly thought out this detail. He was pursing his lips and nodding in approval.

Mariana asked, "So, are we boyfriend-girlfriend, engaged, married?"

Both Jack and Pablo turned suddenly as they were surprised by her question. She returned their surprised look with hands up, gesturing, "what?" and then said, "We need to have our cover story straight, right?"

Jack saw an opportunity to break the tension. He looked directly at Pablo and said, "I think she's flirting with me."

"Si. It does seem like it. Mariana, I must warn you, I think that Jack Kelly will break your heart."

Jack and Pablo laughed heartily, like old friends with many shared experiences.

"Knock it off you two!" She said as a blush came over her face. The banter lifted her spirits a little as it effectively distracted her from her present reality.

Jack held up his hands in surrender and continued.

"It's a good point that she makes. Not married - different last names and too easy to check records. Not engaged, no ring." Then he looked her in the eye. "Just a girl I met in Florida. We had a short fling, and she decided to hop on and sail with me for a bit."

Pablo answered, "Yes, that's the one. It looks and feels right. Where did you meet?"

Mariana took this one.

"The pub in the harbor. My favorite song was playing, and Jack asked me to dance."

She looked at him romantically.

"What's your favorite song?" Jack asked.

"Don't Do Me Like That."

"You know," Pablo interjected, "there's a future for both of you in my business. I need smart people who can think on their feet."

Jack smiled and shook his head.

“Let’s not get ahead of ourselves, Pablo.”

“Ah, but you didn’t say no… So, you will at least consider it?”

“I guess at this point in my life, everything is on the table.”

“And what about you, Mariana?” Pablo asked her.

“I guess at this point in *my* life… I’m just along for the ride.”

Pablo nodded with some satisfaction. Over time, he hoped to bring both of them into his operation. He had vastly different reasons for favoring Mariana and Jack, and he had plans and desires he could not yet reveal. The incident with Diego seemed to have moved his plans along faster, and this pleased him greatly. There would still have to be tests of loyalty. While he sensed progress breaking down the captain, he still saw walls of resistance but could see them starting to crumble. *A little more time, he will come around.* He had forgiven Mariana for running once; he could not do it again. She would have to prove her commitment to him, or he knew that he’d have to kill her. *If that happens, it will break my heart in a way that will never heal.*

25

After they had dropped off Pablo, Jack and Mariana proceeded to the boatyard. Just like in Florida, they received a very warm welcome from the yard manager. It seemed as if Pablo was connected everywhere, and Jack was experiencing the kind of influence that money and power wielded. When someone knew that he was with Pablo, he was treated with respect and deference. Jack was beginning to enjoy this new feeling of importance that stemmed out of his relationship with Pablo, and he was becoming less concerned about the criminal implications.

Windborne was lifted out and put on stands while Jack reviewed the list of damages that had to be addressed. Pablo had instructed both Jack and the yard that no expense was to be spared.

Two armed men appeared and took up station in the yard. *Pablo's guys,* Jack thought. He mused about the irony of leaving his boat with criminals knowing it would be safe in his absence.

With the boat tucked away in the yard, Jack and Mariana grabbed their duffle bags and called a taxi that took them to the hotel where Pablo had booked a single room for the purportedly dating couple.

As the car pulled into the big circular driveway they were struck with the majesty of the building. In the middle of the driveway there stood a huge, tiled fountain, surrounded by vibrantly colored flowering plants. The building was only two stories and was built in a U-shape around a courtyard with tiled patios, flowers, and deep green foliage.

The historic hotel had stood for over three centuries serving to house priests and politicians, first as a school and church, then as a governor's mansion. Now it served tourists, which seemed almost an insult to its rich heritage. The Spanish-Colonial architecture was easily seen in the lush courtyard and majestic colonnades supporting the roof over the entryway. A tall bell tower stood out on the end of the building where a church still held daily services, harkening back to the days when its purpose was more fitting to its majesty.

"Wow," said Mariana as she took it all in.

"Wow, indeed," said Jack. "I could get used to this. My boat repairs are paid for and I'm waiting in the lap of luxury."

"Careful, Jack. It's a very slippery slope."

"I know, but... why should I care - why should you care?"

"He gives you all of this," she motioned to the hotel, "but he robs you of your soul."

"I don't think I have a soul anymore," Jack said slowly and solemnly. "I lost it in the Stream."

Mariana tenderly took his hand for a moment before Jack pulled away to pay the driver. They slid out of the taxi and made their way to the front desk, waving off eager bellhops ready to help them with their small duffle bags.

"Checking in for Jack Kelly," he said as they stepped up to the front desk.

"Welcome to Paraíso, Mr. Kelly."

"Thank you."

"Your room is paid in full; I'll just need your identification and a credit card for incidentals."

Jack fished out his wallet and removed his Florida driver's license and credit card embossed with the name *Windborne Escapes, LLC,* and handed it to the young woman. As she began the process of verifying the information, he turned to Mariana and said, "Let's get ripped tonight."

She looked at him quizzically, surprised by the suddenly buoyant and collegiate tone in his voice. "Ok," she said as she stifled a laugh.

Jack turned back to the front desk, "If I want to party like a pirate and stumble home, where would I go?"

The clerk stopped her work and looked up at him with wide eyes, as if to plead, *please take me with you!* "Oh, you've got to go to *The Pirates Den.* They have over a hundred different kinds of rum, an axe throwing board, and a plank that drops you into the bay – you know, as in walk the plank?"

"Wow," said Mariana, "that sounds a little over-the-top."

"I think it sounds perfect!" Jack said as he suddenly put an arm around Mariana's waist and pulled her in close to him. "And you, my pirate queen shall accompany me. Those that don't bow down before you, will be cut down with my sword!"

Mariana and the front desk clerk laughed at Jack's theater. He held on to Mariana just long enough to signal to her that it wasn't all for show – he wanted her that close to him. She'd felt the sexual tension building but had done her best to stay out of that net. Now, she was exhausted, and her defense mechanisms were breaking down. Half of her wanted to sleep for two days and the other half wanted to tear up the town and then tear into Jack. The latter half was winning.

The young woman interrupted Jack's gaze into Mariana's eyes.

"Well, it sounds like you'll have a heck of night then! Here is your card and license."

She handed him two brass room keys.

"These are your keys, you're on the second floor at the top of that staircase and to the left." she said while pointing to a wide, tiled staircase.

"Is there anything else I can help you with today?"

"Not unless you can talk me out of the hangover that's coming my way tomorrow morning," Jack smiled at her. "Thank you," he looked at her name tag, "Isabella."

"My pleasure, sir. Enjoy your stay on the island."

Jack and Mariana turned and walked up the stairs, down the hallway, and into their room.

It was well appointed with rich, wooden Spanish style furniture. Rough-sawn, exposed beams supported the plaster ceiling, and door arches were lined with hand painted Moroccan tiles. The room opened up onto a deck which overlooked the inside courtyard and fountain.

"Wow. Could we just move in here?" asked Mariana.

"Yeah, you took the words right out of my mouth."

"How about a shower and a nap, then grab a bite to eat and go find our inner pirate?" Jack asked her.

She thought for a moment before she answered, then said, "Did you want to do that shower solo or with your pirate queen?"

Jack was somehow both surprised and not surprised at the same time. He'd certainly felt it coming, but it was the way that she tenderly took his hand in the taxi when he was feeling so lost. It was as if she had grabbed the tiller and turned him onto a new heading. It had been six months of feeling like there was a whirlpool inside of him that was dragging him to the bottom of the sea, and Mariana broke that spell, albeit by casting a new one on him.

"I think that a pirate captain and a pirate queen should always shower together." He leaned in closer as if to kiss her, then half smiled and said, "It's important to save water on a boat."

She playfully smacked him, then pulled him in with her long, tan, strong arms, and kissed him deeply. Pulling away for a moment, she said, "I've wanted to do that since we were on the canal."

"Why didn't you?"

"I didn't want to be unprofessional. Why didn't you kiss me?"

"Who says I wanted to?" Jack quipped.

"You're not as good as you think you are at hiding it. Your eyes said it - you don't think I noticed you watching me?"

She kissed him again.

"I didn't want to be the guy that hired a woman for crew and then hit on her… I've heard the stories."

"You're not that guy, and I'm not that girl. We're grownups, and we don't have to let all the fucked-up rules of society rule us. Plus, I'm the queen and I'm in charge now, not you," she said playfully.

He wrapped his arms around her and kissed her for a long time.

"I don't know if I can give you more than a night, Mariana."

"Who says I want more than a night, Jack. Let's just be here, pirates hell-bent on having a good time. No rules, no judgements, no self-pity, no reflection."

"There's gotta be one rule," said Jack in a serious tone.

"What?"

He pulled her in tightly again, "I must insist that you call me Captain."

She grabbed the collar of his shirt and said, "How dare you talk to your pirate queen that way!" Then she pushed him away, turned and started to walk to the bathroom as she let her threadbare cut-off denim shorts fall to the ground. He lost his breath at the first glimpse of her bare ass above her long, tanned legs. She looked back at him as he stood and stared at her, and said, "Well? Are you coming, Captain?"

"Yes, my Queen."

26

It was a week of nights that they wouldn't soon forget and now it was quite over. Pablo had mostly kept to himself and attended to business, with people coming and going from his room all day and night. He had taken no time to savor life.

Jack and Mariana had been waist deep in the middle of a fling. They had been having sex around the clock, both of them enjoying a distraction from their grim present. One of them would initiate the act throughout the day and night. Regardless of which one lit the match, the other piled on the fuel to burn. But now, *Windborne* was ready and they had to get back an unwelcomed reality.

Jack tapped on Pablo's door lightly and called out, "Pablo, do you want to have breakfast with us before we go to pick up the boat?"

There was a brief silence, then, "Yes, give me ten minutes, por favor. I'll bang on your door."

"Copy that, Boss."

There it was again. Boss. This wasn't an illegal charter; it was a career. Jack didn't notice it, but his preoccupation with Pablo, pirates, rum, and

Mariana had successfully numbed his memory of Jen for the entire week.

He walked back down the hall to his room as carefree as he had ever been. That was about to end.

"He says ten minutes," said Jack.

"Ten means twenty," Mariana replied. "That's enough time for us to go another round. It'll be harder on *Windborne* – especially as loud as we get. We might as well squeeze in one more quickie."

The mention of *Windborne* switched on all the feelings he had turned off. Her suggestion of sex on the boat brought it all back to him in a flood of emotion and memory. The boat was a shrine to the woman he loved more than all others. Sex on that boat felt like it would be a desecration of something sacred.

He paused while he fished for the right answer.

"That's a hell of an offer, but I honestly don't think I have it in me. I think you're in better shape than me, not to mention a decade or so younger."

He smiled and kissed her forehead.

"Ok, your loss."

Jack shook his head and smiled as she walked off to the bathroom. He sat down at the table and poured another cup of coffee from the fine china pot, and he thought about how much Jen would have enjoyed this place. He could see her hair bouncing in the wind, while her shining eyes stared back at him. Then he found himself in the storm and the boat kept rolling as he thought, *Why did she go on deck first? I should always go on deck first.* Then he recalled the words of caution from Laura's father at the trial: "*I suggest you get some professional help. You look like you are falling apart, and your local reputation in the bar precedes you." Yet here I am, running gold and God knows what else for the cartel. If her father could only see me now.*

He said out loud in a frustrated tone, "Pablo… Fuck. Why did I do this?"

Then his mind went back to sea, to the second storm, where he lingered on Diego's death. Finally, he looked around the room and assessed the sum of his activities over the last six months. Once again, lost in his own thoughts, Jack sat motionless with his gaze fixed on a painted picture of an old mission.

Suddenly, he heard a loud banging on the door.

"Jack! Are you still in there?" It was Pablo.

Mariana appeared in a towel and went to the door while Jack sat still, as if in a trance. She looked at Jack.

"Hey, Jack. Snap out of it."

She'd seen it before on the ICW when he almost hit the dredge, and seeing it again concerned her greatly. She opened the door.

"Mornin'," she said as she smiled pleasantly.

"Good morning, my dear."

He leaned over and kissed her gently on the cheek.

"Mr. Kelly, I hope your appetite is big today! And we have much to discuss once we are underway."

Jack stood up to offer Pablo a seat and some coffee. The men sat down as Mariana returned to the bathroom with her clothes.

"Yeah, I'm ready to get rolling. Although, this was a hell of a nice interruption to the trip. Thank you for the room, Pablo, it was really nice. I think this is the nicest place I've ever stayed."

"My pleasure, Jack. I'm glad to see you refreshed. I think we all needed it after that storm and the unfortunate circumstances with our friend."

"Yeah… Do you ever get used to it, Pablo?"

"Used to what?"

"Death."

"Si. It is like anything else; it becomes part of life."

The men sat silently in contemplation of Pablo's words, and then Pablo asked, "Did the yard provide any details on the repairs?"

"Just the price - thirty thou. Look, Pablo. You don't have to pay me for the charter. This is costing you too much between the two repairs and this…" Jack motioned around the room.

"You are an honest man, Jack Kelly. That is both what I respect about you and what concerns me the most. No, I insist you will be paid in full. Your swift action to repair the hull saved our cargo."

Jack nodded, and said, "Thanks, Pablo."

Mariana reappeared, ready to go.

"Okay, boys, let's roll."

As they left the room and walked down to the hotel restaurant for breakfast, each of them was content in their own way. It was not a feeling that would last.

After they had eaten and packed, Pablo arranged for a car to take them back to the boatyard. As they arrived at the yard, they could see *Windborne* in the water below the lift. Jack and Mariana boarded the boat and began their pre-departure checks, while Pablo went to the office to settle the bill with the manager.

"The boat total is $30,194, the private yard security is $6,000," said the manager.

"And as I instructed, the security was told nothing about *Windborne, yes?"*

"Yes, sir. They were only told that we'd had some vandalism, and they were to call me if there was anything suspicious – and to shoot anyone that tried to enter a boat."

"And what about the rafts?"

"We replaced the one that had been deployed and re-certified the other two. So, you have three in good working order."

"Well done, my friend. My uncle said you were a good and loyal man. Here is an extra five thousand for you."

Pablo counted off the money and placed it in his hand.

"Thank you, sir. My mother needs surgery, and this will pay for it."

"How much is the surgery?"

"Forty-seven hundred dollars."

Pablo reached into his pocket and took out three, one-ounce gold coins.

"At the market rate, these will more than cover the surgery," he said as he started to hand them to the man.

"Oh, no. Sir, I couldn't."

"I insist," he said as he handed him the gold. "I hope the best for your mother. Family is everything, yes?"

"Yes," the manager said with teary eyes.

"You understand that we were never here?"

"I understand completely."

Pablo nodded with approval and turned abruptly to walk out the door without saying goodbye.

In the cockpit of *Windborne*, Mariana whispered, "Jack."

He didn't look up from the line he was coiling.

"Yeah."

"Don't look, but there's a Coast Guard RHIB eyeing us."

Jack looked up.

"Jesus, I said *don't look."*

Jack tried to play it off, but the woman on deck had made eye contact with him, so he nodded in courtesy and continued coiling the line. The rigid hull inflatable boat kept passing by the yard and

Jack started to breathe a sigh of relief until it made a wide turn and headed straight toward their dock.

"Okay," he said to Mariana, "put on your poker face. We're a cruising couple that hit a storm and stopped for repairs. Now we are headed to the British Virgin Islands, after that, wherever the winds take us. You remember the rest, right?"

"Like the back of my hand," she replied.

"What about Pablo?" Jack asked.

"He'll figure it out."

When the boat approached the dock, some of its crew tossed lines to tie off, while others armed with MK18 rifles stepped off just ahead of the boat commander.

"Morning, sir, madame," the lead officer said politely.

"Good morning," Jack said as Mariana nodded to the group.

"We'd like to come aboard and have a look around."

"Welcome aboard," said Jack. "The Coast Guard is always welcome aboard *Windborne."*

"I knew this boat looked familiar - you're Captain Jack Kelly, right?"

Jack's heart sank.

"The one and only," Jack said as he tried to manage a smile.

"I was assigned to *Protector* when we came to your aid in the Stream. I'm sorry for your loss, Captain. I'm Ensign Lopez. Nice to meet you in person."

"It's not Captain, anymore, just Jack. They pulled my ticket."

"Oh, sorry. Well, what brings you to our little slice of paradise here, Jack?"

"Me and my girlfriend, Mariana, were headed to the BVI and we took a direct hit from lightning. We were blown off course a bit. A nice hole below the waterline, comms down, the whole shebang. This seemed like our best option for a haul out and refit."

"Wow, you really don't have very good luck, do you Jack?"

"Tell me about it."

The officer looked up toward the yard and noticed a dark-skinned, well-dressed man in sunglasses looking their way and she pointed toward him.

"Is he with you?"

Jack looked up and saw Pablo. He felt his heart skip a beat. Whatever he said next, and whatever Pablo did next, would determine their fate.

"Nope," Jack replied as he shook his head. "Just us." He motioned to him and Mariana.

Pablo saw this and realized what Jack was doing. But he chose not to turn away as it might create suspicion. Instead, he casually pulled out his phone and called the yard manager.

"This is Pablo. I need you to do something for me. Grab a clipboard, walk over to me, and pretend you are showing me paperwork – not for *Windborne*. Then walk away with me to another boat. If the Coast Guard asks about Windborne, tell them that it's only Jack and Mariana. Quickly."

Within a minute the yard manager was talking to Pablo below the hoist. The officer noticed this and turned her attention back to Jack.

"Grab your documentation and IDs, pull out your safety gear – you know the drill."

She turned to her crew and said, "Petty Officer Davis, go below and have a look around."

Jack was thankful for the humidity; it made his perspiration seem legitimate.

"Sure thing, Ensign," Jack replied.

Ensign Lopez looked back up and could see Pablo talking to another man with a clipboard. After a moment, they walked away together. She wasn't satisfied that the man was not with Jack's group. There was something about the way he had looked down at them that made her suspicious. She started to walk up the ramp, when one of her crew called out.

"Ensign, Commander Jefferson on comms for you."

With apparent frustration that her investigation was being interrupted, she turned and walked back to the RHIB.

Jack disappeared below, and Mariana continued to ready things for the voyage. There was a slim chance she could avoid jail if they got caught, but she didn't want to find out.

Petty Officer Davis began poking around below, looking for anything that might seem out of place or suspicious. Jack was at the nav station, gathering the paperwork.

"Sorry it's a bit disorganized down here – after the storm, we just needed a break, so we've got some work to do once we get underway."

"I've seen worse," the man replied dryly. "Is this blood?"

Jack spun around and tried to play cool. "Blood? Where?"

He pointed to the ladder step going topside. Jack realized that they must have missed it when they cleaned up following Diego's death.

"Yeah, that's mine. I got cut up pretty bad tearing out the wood and glass to get to the hole."

Fortunately, that was true. He held up his hand which was littered with scabbed over cuts.

"Jeez, it looks like you got into a fight with a barracuda."

"Yeah, boat life. Super glamorous, right?"

"Throw in a little grease and diesel and you've got cologne," said the Petty Officer in an attempt at humor.

Jack laughed. Then, in a desperate effort to distract the young man, he nodded up towards Mariana and in a quiet voice said, "You wanna hear something funny?"

"What's that?"

"All of that turns her on."

"What?"

"The smell of grease, diesel, even the blood."

"Are you serious?"

"Yep. She's a wild one," said Jack with a smile.

"Marry her."

"I know, right?"

Then Jack grabbed the paperwork and said, "We'd better get this up to your boss - I don't like it when women are mad at me."

"That makes two of us, Mr. Kelly," he said with a smile.

"Call me Jack."

Jack returned to deck with Petty Officer Davis in tow, who had seemed to show little interest in what was below deck once Jack started talking about Mariana. With the knowledge of her purported deviant sexual appetites, Davis wanted to be above deck where he could get a better look at her, and he turned his attention fully towards Mariana once he was topside.

Ensign Lopez had finished her radio conversation and was back on the dock when Jack came topside. He handed over his ship's documentation, insurance, and both of their passports to her. She looked at them briefly and excused herself to go run them on the computer.

Mariana and Jack tried to nonchalantly go back to their chores to get the boat ready to leave. It was a long ten minutes before Ensign Lopez returned to the boat with a smile.

"Ok, Jack, Mariana. Here are your passports and paperwork. We sure hope that you have better luck on this sail but call us if you need us – we'll be there for you."

"I know you will. That's why I hate leaving U.S. waters, because I feel a lot safer knowing you guys are around."

"Thanks, Cap-" she caught herself, "Jack."

With that, they boarded their boat and sped off to another part of the harbor.

Jack sat down in silence and Mariana did the same. After a minute, he said, "Holy fuck."

"Yeah, that was way too close."

"Call Pablo's cell and tell him that the coast is clear, but let's not take any chances. Let's have the yard run them out to us when we are offshore - just in case they re-board us again."

"Do you think that would happen?" she asked.

"Probably not, but we can't take the risk. We told them that he wasn't with us and if they find him on the boat, they'll know we're lying and hiding something, and they'll rip the boat apart. Tell them we'll call with coordinates once we get underway."

Mariana made the call.

"Jack wants you to stay at the yard and let us get a few miles offshore, then have someone at the yard run you out to meet us. He said if the Coast Guard stops us again and you're on board, they'll search it stem to stern."

"Can I trust you, mija?"

She wasn't surprised by his use of the contracted phrase, *my daughter*.

"Of course, we aren't fools, Don Pablo. We would never steal from you."

The phone was silent for a long moment while Pablo considered his options. He wasn't comfortable letting them sail off with his gold, but he knew Jack was right. Pablo thought, *He is beginning to think like someone operating outside of the law.* This pleased Pablo a great deal.

"Fine, we will do as the Captain suggests."

Just under two hours later, a fast boat dropped Pablo off at the rendezvous point, and the three of them set sail for Colombia. Pablo was relieved that his trust had not been misplaced, and that both of them had shown loyalty to the family. Jack had now passed his second test with Pablo. The first had been his attack on Diego.

As Pablo lay down in his berth, he began to contemplate his plans. *Jack is progressing nicely and seems well suited for the business. Mariana still seems somewhat withdrawn – this is unsatisfactory. I will find a way to pull her in closer. After all, she is the only daughter I will ever have.*

27

It was a week of calm and quiet on all fronts – almost too quiet. There had been no storms, no death, no drama. A dark mood had come over Pablo and he had largely confined himself to his berth, and a sudden awkwardness had overtaken Jack and Mariana. The questions relentlessly compounded in their minds. Were they in a relationship? Friends with benefits? Were they captain and mate? Were they in love or lust? What would happen in Colombia? What would happen after Colombia? What would happen after that? It was a mental contemplation that rivaled the strongest of tides - pulling, pushing, and tugging at them as it came and went. Neither of them had a relationship foundation strong enough to build upon because they were weakened by a past littered with loss and regret. Clinging to each other seemed like a natural option that both of them eschewed. Each day, they would busy themselves with boat chores, and each night, all three of them would quietly retreat to their berths with hardly a word spoken.

Mariana was splicing a dock line when Jack came topside for his watch.

"Hey, Mar. Not too much longer. Pablo told me to put in just off Rincon Del Mar, south of Punta Hacienda. There's a little tip protruding off the point that will protect us from anything coming from the north. The forecast is calm with a high-pressure area sitting over the region, so we should be fine," he said to her. "I forgot to tell Pablo I want a sailor or mariner to stay on the boat – someone that knows boat systems – pass that on for me, would ya?"

"Sure thing, Cap."

There it was - the order and the obedience. They both sensed it, and the questions resumed in their minds.

Jack picked up the cruising guide and began to read the details of the area. He'd heard stories of rocks the size of houses in coastal areas that were yet uncharted and presented a danger to all mariners. He thought, *The vastness of the ocean will not surrender to the human desire for knowledge and control.*

After Jack finished with the cruising guide, he began reading notes online from other cruisers and thought about how much he was enjoying the satellite connection that Pablo had purchased for him. Jack had always been thorough, but after the accident in the Gulf Stream, he became obsessed with details. At times, he would pore over the same section of a chart for hours, as if by peering at it harder, he could discern all of its secrets and protect his passengers.

Mariana returned with a message for Jack. "Pablo says, 'Bueno,' he'll call to have them meet us to unload, and he wants to know the E.T.A."

"This wind is lightening, and I want to drop anchor well before sunset, so let's drop sail and motor in. That will give us a predicable arrival time..." Jack paused and looked at his watch. "Let's call it 4:00 P.M. for anchor down and boat secured."

She nodded before saying, "He's going to have his father's people meet us and help with the offload, then they will take us to the family rancho about an hour outside of town. He said there's going to be a big homecoming celebration, and that we should wear our nicest clothes – of which I have none – so I'm going to pick up a sundress in town on the way."

Jack paused and considered all that she had said. "I don't suppose there is any way we can opt out of this, is there?"

She dropped her gaze to the floor and shook her head. Jack was beginning to fully understand his relationship with Pablo and said nothing more.

"Ok, take the helm and bring her up into the wind. I'll bring in the canvas."

Jack knew that the sails weren't actually made of canvas; like most nautical terms, it was an old term steeped in antiquity. The sails on *Windborne* were made of Dacron; they were new and expensive, and he had Pablo to thank for those too.

Mariana did as she was instructed, stepping behind the helm, turning off the autopilot and then turning *Windborne* up into the wind and just slightly off the wind to take the pressure off the headsail which Jack began to roll up. Once it was secured, he opened the clutch for the main halyard. The well-lubricated sail slugs came down like a guillotine as the weight of the sail and gravity worked in concert together. When the sail was down, Jack cleaned everything up, and turned back to Mariana.

"Give me a heading of 170 degrees. I'm going below to take a short nap – wake me in two hours."

"Aye, Cap" was all that she said.

It hadn't gone unnoticed to her that his orders were cold and mechanical. He wasn't the same Jack Kelly that she'd started to fall for in Puerto Rico, or even the same man that she'd come down the ICW with from Virginia to Fort Lauderdale. This was a new Jack Kelly, distant and detached. She knew that he was in there somewhere, and while she wrestled with her demons, she had just enough strength to help him vanquish a few of his own. Mariana fully understood the powerful magnetism of Pablo and she didn't want to abandon Jack to its forces. Whether it was love, or just her job as first mate, she had a keen sense of loyalty to the captain. As Jack disappeared below, she spoke quietly to herself, "I'm not going to give up so easily, Jack Kelly. It may be too late for me, but it's not too late for you."

As Jack climbed down, he saw Pablo and neither man said a word, not even a nod in acknowledgment. Jack turned and went into his cabin. There was a strange combination of tension and relief building in Jack as they approached the end of the sail. There was still so much unsettled in his mind, the least of which was whether or not he would throw in his lot with Pablo and start running drugs north and gold south, stopping in Puerto Rico to fool around with Mariana. Then the thought occurred to him, *Would Mariana go for any of this?* He doubted it, given her long-standing attempt to be free of Pablo. He drifted off to an uneasy slumber until he heard Mariana's voice calling him back.

"Jack, I've got the point in sight, land ho, Cap."

Jack mumbled a response so that she knew he was awake, and then got up and freshened-up with a face wash and a little hair paste. He was up on deck in five minutes, surveying the land with a monocular. After he'd satisfied his visual sensory input, he went to the chart plotter and zoomed in to a closeup of the bay, then dropped a pin on the chart.

"Mariana, please let Pablo know that we'll be dropping anchor in about forty minutes. Take a short break and grab a snack, then come back up. I'm going to put you on the bow – there may be uncharted rocks or reefs here, and I'd prefer it if we didn't hit one."

"Will do, Jack."

She ducked down below deck as Jack continued to survey the land.

Jack said to himself, "Well, one thing's for sure, we're here – gold and all. I don't know if I'm built for this life… Only one way to find out." His heart rate was increasing with each nautical mile towards shore.

Pablo had assured him that the officials and local police had already been paid and that they would not encounter any inspections or boardings – though that did not include protection from the Colombian Navy. If the Navy boarded them, it would be more complicated and require his father's intervention. It would still all work out, but it would likely include an impound of the boat and a few days in a cell. Jack picked up the monocular and scanned the horizon again, this time in all directions. There was no sign of a naval vessel.

After a while, Mariana came back on deck and headed straight to the bow, she wasn't in the mood for chit-chat, and she knew the drill for bow watch. They were still a couple of miles out, so after preparing the anchor, she plopped down on the deck and dropped her feet over the bow on either side of the boat. It was one of her favorite spots to hang out.

As they approached the bay, Jack canceled the autopilot and began to survey the area he'd selected for the anchorage. He called up to Mariana, "Heads up, we're on the shelf."

She popped up, tightened the strap holding the back of her sunglasses and leaned out over the bow pulpit, peering into the clear water that was still too deep to reveal the bottom. As she did, Jack slowed the boat to five knots, then four, and then down to two knots as they approached the pin. Before he hit the mark, he dropped the engine into neutral and drifted up to the location slowly, keeping an eye on his depth finder. Then, taking one last look around, he called out, "Drop 110!"

Mariana called back, "Dropping 110 feet."

She hit the anchor remote button marked "down" and the windlass let go and sent the anchor to the seabed. Once the chain showed slack, she gave a thumbs up to Jack. He put *Windborne* in reverse and started to back down on the anchor to set it in place. When he felt the resistance as the boat came to a stop, he found a stationary bearing on shore and sighted it with his thumb. *Not moving. Looks like we got a good bite.* He gave Mariana a thumbs up in return and reached down to shut off the engine. Mariana left the bow and went about getting the lines and ladders ready that they would soon need.

Pablo appeared on deck and was in an incredibly good mood.

"¡Hola! ¿Como estás?" shouted Pablo.

"Nice of you to join us, Pablo," said Jack with welcoming sarcasm. "Did you call your peeps?"

"Yes, my friend. A team is standing by onshore. Tonight there is to be a great celebration at my father's rancho."

"Sounds fun," Jack lied boldly. "I'll head below to put on my best outfit."

Pablo nodded and smiled.

Jack caught Mariana's eye and winked at her before disappearing below deck. *What the hell was that?* She wondered. *Is this an onshore-only fling?* She was definitely into him but questioned her ability to carry her baggage as well as his – he certainly didn't seem capable of carrying his own. She continued with her chores until all of the lines were made-well and the port-lights were open for ventilation. The boat was ship-shape, and it brought her a small measure of comfort to control this one small thing in her very out of control universe.

By the time Mariana reappeared on deck, the crew was arriving in several small boats and preparing to receive the cargo. Pablo was shouting instructions in Spanish as the seven men scrambled up the boarding ladders on port and starboard, and into the cockpit. Three of the men dispersed to different sections of the boat and stood watch with assault weapons at the ready. They wore military-style body armor and carried enough spare magazines to engage in a lengthy firefight.

The first thing that Pablo did was to give each of them a small pouch with ten gold coins. He knew that seeing this enormous amount of gold would make them desire it, so he preemptively worked to ease the strain of that desire. He also knew that someday he might need them in his corner, and they would remember his kindness.

The storage compartments were opened quickly with a battery-operated angle cutter, revealing the blood-stained treasure that lined the once virgin hull of *Windborne.* Four men began to offload the twenty-five gold bars. Each bar weighed twenty-seven pounds and was worth more than three-billion pesos in Colombia. The men formed a chain stretching from below decks to the transfer boat and passed each bar up until the compartments were emptied. Then, they took the artwork, which was carefully secured in tubes, along with small boxes of expensive jewelry, and a small armory of guns and ammunition, and continued the effort until the boat was cleansed from the stain that had darkened her.

Jack's blemish was still darkening inside of him while his outside appearance covered it up. He came back out on deck, looking sharp in his best khakis and a Hawaiian print button down shirt, and with his feet shod for the first time in months with a pair of new topsiders that he'd picked up before they left Florida. Unnoticed to Jack, Mariana looked at him up and down slowly. Despite her frustration, she couldn't deny the attraction.

Pablo said impatiently, "You look very nice, Jack. Now, are we ready to go?"

"Yes, Don Pablo."

Jack's use of the word "Don" caught the attention of some of the men, as it was normally reserved for Pablo's father. But Pablo himself bathed in the humble reverence offered by Jack.

Pablo nodded, and said authoritatively, "Let's go!" He then turned and boarded the lead boat, which immediately pulled away from *Windborne.*

Jack turned to the man who was staying behind, and asked him, "You're good with all the systems?"

"Yes, my father sailed as a captain and I grew up on sailboats," he replied in good, but heavily accented English.

"Okay. I'm sure you know how to get ahold of us if there are any problems or questions, yes?"

"Sí, Capitán."

"Thank you," Jack said to the man as he turned toward the ladder. As Mariana prepared to step down to the second boat, Jack held onto her arm gently and said, "I'm sorry I've been such an…" Jack paused as he searched for the word.

"Ass?" she replied.

"Sure, that works. You might have to expound on it a bit," he said.

"Oh, I will," she said with both finality and humor before turning to board the small boat that floated below them.

Jack took one last, long look around to ensure *Windborne* was secure, and then turned to leave her at rest. He wished that he could rest with her, but in his soul brewed a hurricane that he felt would surely end in his destruction.

28

Mariana's shopping trip in town had only taken about twenty minutes. She wasn't picky, and she had a nearly perfect body; everything looked good on her. She'd made Jack play the approving boyfriend role outside of a changing room. Each time she came out, he'd say the same things: wow, amazing, stunning... He meant every word. Soon, she was dressed like a wealthy tourist, and her dirty, blood-stained clothing was tied up in a plastic bag.

After a bumpy, forty-minute ride in an eighty-thousand-dollar four-wheel drive pickup truck, the driver turned off to a private road that was marked as such in both English and Spanish. It was paved and perfectly maintained - not a pothole in sight. About a hundred yards past the turn off was a heavy, steel gate that seemed almost irrelevant because it was guarded by men in full military tactical gear and armed with automatic weapons. The driver waved at them as the truck approached and came to a stop. Greetings were exchanged and the gate was opened quickly. The road continued to wind up a hill that was covered in lush vegetation for the next three miles, until it finally opened up onto a huge, grass-covered valley.

As the truck came out of the foliage covered road, Jack could see two large buildings about a half mile apart, and several smaller buildings surrounding the larger ones.

"I've only heard about this place," said Mariana. "The description of paradise didn't do it justice."

"Yeah, wow. This is amazing," Jack replied.

Cattle grazed peacefully as the truck rolled down the road. The shadows cast by the falling sun began to create contrasts of dark and light. Jack looked at the patches of light and reflected on this strange position in which he found himself. *There is no light in this place,* he thought. Yet here he was, by deceit and denial. He knew that he had to make the best of it.

He was beginning to see that an expert trapper had perfectly placed the bait. Jack had simply walked in, picked it up, and then watched as the steel door slammed shut. He was beginning to understand why Mariana felt the way that she did, and why she had gone to such great lengths to free herself from Pablo. Yet he was conflicted; part of him was beginning to accept his circumstances. *Fate?* He wondered.

The driver, who had been silent the entire ride, began to speak in perfect, unaccented English.

"The casa on the left belongs to Don Julio, the one on the right, the new one, that's the one that the Don built for Pablo. I think it is very beautiful, wouldn't you agree?"

"Wow," said Jack. "Yeah, that's a hell of a nice gift from a father to his son.

"Don Julio would never admit it, but Pablo is his pride and joy. He always goes on about his son's exploits in America. He is so thrilled to have him home. A tip if I may offer one… The Don loves to hear people compliment Pablo and it's important to *always* be in his good graces."

Something about the way he emphasized the word '*always'* stood out to Jack as if to reinforce there was never room for deviation from this absolute truth.

"Appreciate the advice," Jack lied. He wanted to ask the driver if the Don had written a manual for raising a sociopath. To find out if Don Julio had forgotten to teach his son a single moral principle. To learn the mystery of why this man felt that human life was a disposable commodity as long as it served the purpose of gaining money, gold, or power. Jack was smart enough to know that any of those questions would likely result in a bullet to the back of his skull. He looked over at Mariana and just shook his head slightly in bewilderment. Her reply was silent; the knowing look of someone that understood so completely that words were unnecessary, for they could never describe the knowledge of her soul.

By the time Jack had cleared his mind and reset his outward persona, the truck came into a huge circle, with a giant fountain surrounded by lush bougainvillea.

"All right, my friends, here we are."

"Thanks for the lift," said Mariana.

He pointed to a small casa on the right, "That's my home, if you need anything at all, don't hesitate. I'll be around for a few days."

"Appreciate it," said Jack.

"Oh, and if you want to take a horseback ride, just let someone know."

"Cool, might take you up on that," Mariana said with a hint of enthusiasm that Jack hadn't heard since Puerto Rico.

As they stepped out of the truck and grabbed their duffle bags from the back, they heard Pablo's booming voice.

"¡Hola! ¡Bienvenido! Mi casa es su casa."

Jack and Mariana turned to greet him.

"Hey, Pablo," Mariana said as she leaned in for a hug.

"Hello, Boss," said Jack. "Any chance you've got any tequila laying around? I've been cravin' it since my feet touched land."

Pablo seemed pleased with Jack's request and said, "See? Colombia is already working her magic on you, Captain. Oh, my friend, if tequila is what you seek, then you are in for a treat, my father's collection is quite extensive. You will be amazed!"

"Well, since all I need is here, I guess I'll be moving into one of these casas," Jack jokingly replied as he motioned around the ranch.

"Don't worry, Jack. When we are done, you can have a beautiful home of your own, right over there,"

Pablo pointed to a spot that looked like paradise to Jack. Then, he turned and said, “Come along now!”

Pablo walked a few feet ahead of them and they all stopped when a servant interrupted to ask a question. Pablo turned to them, saying, “One moment,” as he stepped into another room with the servant.

“He’s serious, you know that right?” Mariana asked Jack quietly.

“About what?”

“The house.”

“Really?”

“Yeah, he doesn’t let people into his circle easily, but once you’re in, you’re well cared for.”

“So, why’d you leave then?” Jack asked her.

“Complete fealty is a stiffer price than you might imagine.”

“But the draw is powerful, right?” Jack asked.

“It’s intense. Not just the trappings - it’s his personality. When he loves you, you feel like you’re the only one in the world. It’s intoxicating,” she said as her gaze shifted from him into the distance. “When he’s displeased, you feel as if you would do anything to win his favor back.”

Pablo walked back into the hallway and saw them talking.

“Am I interrupting?” he asked them.

“No, we were just complimenting the architecture – it’s amazing,” said Jack. The lying was getting easier.

The home was a traditional Spanish-Colonial style, with thick alabaster adobe walls and terracotta roof tiles. The exposed wood beams that supported the roof came out through the adobe, and traditional wooden shutters graced the windows. The home was enormous; Jack guessed that it was at least 20,000 square feet.

"Wait until you see the home my father built for me - but not before tequila!"

He turned and led them through a large double door made from thick, solid, rough sawn oak. The floor was traditional red-clay tile pavers with hand painted ceramic tile inlays every few feet, and the walls displayed oil paintings worth more than the home that Jack had grown up in.

"This is *really* nice," Jack wasn't lying now. "I could live here and never cross an ocean again."

"Well, that's the plan, Jack. We will do all of our work, and then we will have our beautiful homes and gardens... and a dog. I think I'd like to get an Australian Shepard. What about you Jack, do you want a dog?"

"Yeah, I'd like a dog," he replied.

"What about me?" Mariana asked playfully as if she had been forgotten.

He turned to her and put his hands on her shoulders.

"For you, my dear daughter, you will have not one, but five dogs, or ten, or a hundred!" He laughed wildly at the idea of a hundred dogs. "But no one gets a dog until after our work is done. But enough talk of work.

It's time to drink in celebration! You will all meet my father soon, and he will see why I have chosen you to be my consejeras di confianza."

Mariana looked surprised, "Your trusted advisors? Us?"

"Yes, my dear, yes."

"You might want to rethink that, Pablo," Jack said with a wry smile.

"Enough of this joking around," Pablo said with a smile on his face, we have serious work to do in selecting our tequila!"

The three of them laughed like old friends, and it seemed that Jack and Mariana were comfortable and content, if only for the moment.

The room they entered was lined with more bottles of tequila than Jack could count. The bottles were housed on old, library style shelves, with a rolling ladder that went down each wall. Many of the bottles were hand painted, in the Mexican tradition of Dia de los Muertos, the Day of the Dead. *How fitting,* thought Jack.

"Here is the menu in English. We have them in six languages for guests because my father is very detail oriented. That's an important quality for men in our business. I'll get one of the staff to serve us, make yourselves at home.

After Pablo had left the room, Jack turned to Mariana and said, "I could get used to this."

"No, you can't," she said sternly.

"Why not?"

"I know you Jack, and you won't pay the price."

"Haven't I already paid enough?"

"You don't get it. It's not a price you pay once, it's a bill that's perpetually due on demand."

Jack remained silent. He knew that she was right. He actually hated Pablo, but he had some kind of mixed-up love-hate relationship with him. He also knew that he was the one who had surrendered himself to this life, and part of him didn't even care. The dead part. The part that died in the Gulfstream.

"Fuck it. What's the difference? We're always paying a price; we might as well have good tequila to drink."

"Jack," she pleaded. "Come on, this isn't you."

"How do you know who I am? You think that because we've sailed together and had a few good rolls in the sack that you know me? You don't know anything about me. You have no idea how desperately I've wanted to live in a bottle of rum - or shove a gun barrel into my mouth. You don't fucking get it sometimes, kid."

"I'm not a kid."

"You're a lot younger than I am."

"You have no idea what you're talking about. This isn't playing pirate, Jack, it's a life headed nowhere except a soulless existence, a jail cell, or if you're really lucky, an early grave."

"What makes you think my existence isn't soulless now? It sure feels that way since I lost Jen."

"Jack, I'm not trying to minimize your pain. But I'm telling you that whatever you think this…" she paused as she pointed around the room at the bottles on the wall, "...is now, it's not this. It's death, it's harming others, it's unquestioned loyalty to the king, and death if you fail him. You saw what he did to Diego over a few gold bars."

Pablo had overheard the last few sentences in the hallway as he approached, and it darkened his bright countenance. But he understood her words in a personal way that he could never reveal to her. For after all, that's how he felt about his own father, in whose house he now stood. Mariana was right and Pablo knew it. Don Julio had required all of that from him over and over since his 16th birthday. He knew that as quickly as he had killed Diego, his own father would kill him. He was sad because he knew this about his father. He was sad because he knew this about himself. He was sad because his friends knew this about *him.* He genuinely cared about Mariana a great deal, as if she were his own child. And he cared about Jack too – in a different way. But she was right, he thought, *I'll kill them without regret if they cross me.*

29

The tequila had done its work, and all of their cares had melted away. Now, they were seated at one end of an enormous table built to entertain thirty people, waiting for Don Julio to make his appearance at dinner. The staff had said that he had been spending more time alone in his room lately, and it concerned them, though they had been afraid to say anything about it. The smells from the kitchen were heavenly and the alcohol had triggered their appetites. Pablo sat at the head of the table, and on that same end of the table Jack sat across from Mariana. There was a table setting at the far end of the huge table for Don Julio, and according to Pablo, no one except him could occupy that seat. Once, as a young man, he had tried to sit there and received a good beating for his insolence.

"My father will be joining us soon," he said to the two of them. Then he yelled in Spanish to an unseen staff member, "¡Arepas, pronto!"

"Pablo, I've never heard you mention your mother. Forgive me if it's impolite for me to ask," Jack asked in a deferential tone.

"No, it's ok, Jack. Friends should know these things. I'm sad to say that she is no longer with us, Jack. She died soon after I left for America – which my father ordered me to do. The doctor said she died of a broken heart." Pablo looked upward, made the sign of the cross and then blew a kiss to the heavens.

"I'm sorry for your loss," said Jack.

Mariana nodded in agreement as the chips and salsa appeared on the table.

"You know the pain of this type of loss, Jack, which is one of the many things I appreciate about you."

"Thank you, Pablo."

Mariana seemed uncomfortable anytime there was a moment where the two men bonded. Jack noticed it, but couldn't understand if it was her concern for him, or her jealousy of the new relationship between them. On the one hand, it seemed like she hated Pablo; on the other, she was like an actress in a soap opera who had been playing the role for a long time and could easily ad lib her lines when necessary.

"You both have suffered tremendous losses, and it hurts you both deeply," she said with empathy and compassion.

"Thank you, dear," said Pablo.

"You are a very special person, Mariana," Jack said with deep emotion as he stared at her.

She blushed, uncomfortable with the sudden and intense attention from both men.

A servant entered the room and spoke loudly in English.

"Please rise to greet Don Julio."

The group stood up and waited as the big man entered the room. He stood well over six feet, with very broad shoulders, large arms, hands like sledgehammers, and a small waist for a man of his size and age. His dark, wavy hair was brushed back and held in place with hair gel and his face showed the scars of a man that had literally fought his way to the top.

As Pablo, Jack, and Mariana stepped away from the table and toward the center of the room to greet him, he stopped and waited as a king holding court. Pablo was first in line to pay homage.

"Don Julio, I am honored to be in your presence again."

Then, the man who Mariana had never seen defer to anyone, bent over slightly, took his hand, and kissed his ring.

Don Julio took Pablo by the shoulders and stood him up, gazing intently into his eyes. "My son, it is so good to see your face in my home. I wish you to never leave again."

"Gracias, Don."

"You will no longer call me Don. From this day forward you will call me father, again, as you did when you were a boy."

Pablo's face lit up.

"Thank you, Do-," he interrupted his error, "Thank you, Father, thank you."

He wanted to grab the big man and hug him tightly, but he knew this would not be acceptable. Instead, after this moment that he'd longed for his entire life, he dutifully stood aside and began the introductions. His father had taught him manners – manners drilled into him at the end of a bull whip the few times he'd forgotten them.

"Father, may I present the lovely Mariana Hansen."

Don Julio looked at the tall woman almost eye to eye, and then embraced her lightly. "I have heard so much about you over the years, I am delighted to finally meet you in person, Mariana."

"Thank you, Don. It's my honor to be here, in your home, in the presence of such a great man."

Don Julio smiled at his son, "This one, watch out for her. She is more beautiful than any Greek Goddess and has the silver tongue of an Irish Princess." Then he turned back to her and said, "Men must melt in your presence, mija!"

He looked at Jack and said, "This must be the pirate scoundrel you call Jack Kelly!" He laughed loudly as he thrust out one hand to shake and put the other on Jack's shoulder.

"I am, sir."

"My son says there is no captain better than you!"

"Well, he's been most gracious and kind to me, Padrino."

Don Julio looked impressed at Jack's use of the word Godfather, and he glanced approvingly at his son.

Pablo smiled and said, "The good Captain has been working on his Spanish."

The Don nodded and then said, "I've had them roast a suckling pig for you, my friends! We will stuff our faces until we cannot even talk or walk! Please sit down, enjoy."

Then, after all the warmth and welcoming, the big man took his seat at the far end of the table, twenty feet from his guests. The king will always sit on his throne.

Talk of pleasure and happiness soon drifted into talk of money and business. The conversation became dominated by the father and the son, leaving Jack and Mariana eating while barely looking up from their plates. The instructions were explicit, and Jack heard the words that finally snapped him out of the pirate fantasy with which he'd been having casual intercourse.

"The cocaine will be loaded onto *Windborne,* and we will add more sailboats to the fleet if this run is successful," said Don Julio. Then, he looked directly at Jack, "And I will hold you personally responsible if anything happens to my shipment." Next, he looked at Mariana, "She will pay any price for your mistakes, Captain."

Pablo said, "Look, Jack, I know this is not what you thought would happen, but now you see that you can have a nice life here in Colombia. You don't have to sail the boats, you can hire other captains and run the operation at sea. This is why I so carefully selected you; I know that you have this ability."

Jack wanted to scream, but instead he looked over at Mariana and she shook her head almost imperceptibly, while mouthing the word 'later.' He knew that she was right and looked back down at his plate.

"I do like it here in Colombia, Pablo; I like it a lot," said Jack.

Jack managed a smile at the two men and returned to his meal. He knew that he was trapped in a cage which he had helped to build. His earlier desperation to fix *Windborne* in Norfolk and escape had been replaced by an even greater desperation. *I have to figure a way out of this…*

Mariana looked on, unphased by this new revelation. Her own deep desperation remained, and she had felt that way for a very long time.

30

Mariana sat alone in the dark listening to Jack sleeping. She could tell that it was an unrestful sleep as he fidgeted and murmured. It took no stretch of her imagination to think of what disturbed the man; she didn't sleep for many of the same reasons.

She thought about the catapult that had freed her from Pablo the first time, *Was it fate or chance?*

One morning, during her daily stop at a coffee house, she met a woman that was a Chief Stewardess on a superyacht that was preparing to leave for a Mediterranean cruise. There was something about the way the woman described the life onboard that made her yearn for her freedom from Pablo.

In a moment of brave spontaneity, Mariana asked, "Do you need any more crew?"

"Funny you should ask. Just this morning, one of my crew found out that her mom has cancer. She had to resign and fly home. Maybe the universe arranged this meeting," said the Chief Stew as she smiled warmly.

"Yeah, maybe. I'm looking to expand my horizons a bit. I've had friends work these kinds of jobs and they love it."

"It's not sunshine and sandy beaches – at least not for the crew. You get that, right?"

"It's a job, not a vacation," said Mariana.

The woman laughed at her response, and said, "I like that, I may borrow it for my interviews."

Mariana smiled.

"Sure."

The Chief continued, "I like you, what's your name?"

"Mariana Hansen."

"Nice to meet you, Mariana. My name is Chloe, the boat is *Destiny,* do you know where the *Shoreline End* docks are?"

"Yeah, I know that area. I run down that way."

"Great. Show up with some casual clothes and a comfortable pair of white boat sneakers, along with your toiletries, books, and what not. We'll provide your uniform and everything else you'll need. We're heading out for a shakeout cruise in the morning, and we'll give you a working interview. If it works out, you will need to attend Standards of Training Certification and Watchkeeping – STCW as it's known in the industry. How's that sound?"

"It sounds amazing!" Mariana exclaimed.

"Don't you want to know about the pay or hours?"

Mariana shook her head and said, "Nope. I'm sure it's fair."

"The STCW costs about a thousand bucks; can you cover it?"

"Yeah, I stashed away my tips from my waitressing job," Mariana lied.

"I think you'd be a good fit. I need someone who's chill; sometimes there's too much drama on yachts."

"I've seen the reality shows – is it really like that?"

"Well, not that bad. But bad enough, and I don't like drama. Can you follow orders?"

Mariana almost laughed out loud, "Yeah, I can follow orders."

"Okay then, Mariana, we'll see you at the dock in the morning. 8:00 A.M. sharp."

"I can't wait!" Mariana said eagerly. "You have no idea of how much this will change my life!"

Even the name of the yacht seemed like a sign to her. *Destiny… Perhaps it is.*

Over the course of the next few weeks, Mariana feigned illness and then a family emergency to explain her absence from Pablo's circle. She'd always been a good, loyal soldier, so he had no concerns about her absence.

The captain and crew of *Destiny* loved her work ethic, and she was clearly a good fit for boat life. They welcomed her into their circle and helped her learn the ropes. A few weeks later, she quietly said goodbye to her mom and slipped away into a world of water. When Pablo learned of her disappearance, at first, he was furious, but eventually he was saddened.

After a year on *Destiny*, she decided to work toward a captain's license and learn to sail. The Captain of *Destiny* used his network to get her a job on a ninety-foot sailing yacht as a deckhand, and she began cruising the world on a billionaire's yacht. After crossing the Atlantic, cruising the Caribbean, and trekking up the U.S. coast to Newport, Rhode Island, Mariana was ready to start working on her Merchant Mariner Credential. She left the yacht, rented a run-down apartment in South Boston, and started taking courses at a local school for mariners.

While it was now *her* life, it was still a life on the run, and it was taking a toll on her. She felt like she'd hit an invisible wall, as if she'd been wrestling with God and losing. She was tired of constantly looking over her shoulder, and her mind was weary from wondering what would happen if she ever met up with Pablo or his crew – she knew the price she would pay for her transgressions.

After a few months onshore, she needed a break. She was getting homesick and decided to risk a trip back home to see her mom. She was on a train headed south when she saw Jack's posting for the run to Fort Lauderdale. It seemed like an easy way to pick up a few bucks, get some smaller yacht experience, and slip into town quietly. Mariana could never have guessed that all of her efforts would be undone by her own choices, and that destiny – if indeed it existed – was taking her back to the very man she had fought so hard to escape.

As she lay in the room next to Jack, she almost laughed out loud when she recalled the Chief Stew's question about following orders. *Yeah, Chloe, I guess I know how to follow orders. Pablo's, yours, Jack's – I'm tired of following orders.*

Mariana began to go back further in her mind, and the better part of the night would be sleepless as she tormented herself about all of the short-sighted decisions of an awkward teenage girl who couldn't seem to fit in anywhere. She had made the trade to fit in and find acceptance but had fatally failed to recognize the cost. *Such is the vantage point of youth,* she thought.

It was my 21st birthday, you son of a monster. How could you have done that to me? Mariana almost screamed the words out loud as she clenched her fists in the dark room. Sweat began to form on her brow as she recalled the day that had deepened her relationship with Pablo, the day that the construction of her prison was completed.

Pablo invited the entire neighborhood to her birthday party. Friends, family, local shopkeepers, police officers, and his crew, all gathered together to celebrate. The tequila and beer flowed to the adults and scheming teens, while the younger children overdosed on cola, cake, and candy. Pablo's home was decorated with festive streamers, balloons, and piñatas.

Now, looking back, she thought, *You fucker! I hate you for what you did!*

As the party was winding down, he called her into his study.

"I have a very special gift for you, Mariana."

From his desk drawer he removed an ornate, hand carved wooden box and handed it to her. What Mariana saw inside puzzled her greatly. It was stunningly beautiful. The gemstones looked expensive as she admired them, but the item itself confounded her as she thought, *Why a jewel studded dagger for my birthday?*

"It is beautiful, yes?"

"Yes, Padrino, but why did you choose a dagger?"

He walked back to his desk and pulled out the .45 caliber pistol that his own father had given him.

"Do you remember this gun, my dear girl?"

She nodded and waited. Sometimes he paused when he spoke, and she'd seen him pistol whip men for interrupting his train of thought.

"On my 16th birthday, my father, the great Don Julio gave me this pistol. It was not entirely a gift, it was more of a key, a key into his world. As you my dear are like my own daughter, I wanted to give you the same gift that my father gave to me."

"Wow, I'm so honored that you've included me in this tradition, Padrino."

"Please, when we are alone, just call me, Papa."

Her eyes began to tear up at this gesture of love from the man who seemed to be everything. Since her own father had died, Pablo had rushed in like the wind to fill the void.

"You said it was a key, what do you mean by that, Papa?"

"Well, it is yours to keep regardless of your next decision. If you decide to go down the path that I offer to you, it will bring you fully into my family and my business. I had no such choice; I was ordered to do so. But every parent wants things to be better for their children than it was for them, so respectfully, I have improved on my own father's path."

"I thought I came into the family the day I got this."

Mariana displayed the tattoo on her wrist that he had given her on the day she shot Doug. She waited patiently for his answer as he studied her face carefully, and then put his hands on her already strong, broad shoulders.

"Yes, you did, dear. But everyone that works for me gets one of those, not everyone gets one of these."

Pablo pulled back his shirt to reveal a colorful crest tattooed over his heart.

"This is my family crest, if you accept my assignment, you will get one of these, you will become untouchable. You will become one of my heirs as I have no children of my own."

"What do you want me to do?"

"There is a man that keeps great security, but he has a weakness for beautiful women. I think you can lure him into the bedroom. *Before* he defiles you, you will put this dagger in his neck and end his rat-life. Then my dear daughter, you will be as deadly as you are beautiful. That is why I chose this dagger for you. See how beautiful and deadly it is? Just as you will be my dear. And I will be so proud of you on that day."

Back in the room, Mariana continued her dance with the past. Recalling her turmoil as she had walked out of Pablo's home that day with a twenty-thousand-dollar jewel studded dagger that would soon be stained with a man's blood.

She began to weep silently at what she had become. *Is there any way I can ever escape him?* She scratched violently at the family crest on her chest as if she could remove the tattoo with her own fingernails. Then, she heard Jack scream, mercifully lifting her out of her thoughts.

"Jack, wake up, you're having another nightmare."

He sat up in bed and rubbed his eyes, wet with tears.

"The storm again?" She asked him.

"Yeah, Jen was drowning, and my arms were frozen, I couldn't reach her. I couldn't save her."

"You loved her so much. She was lucky to have you in her life."

"Lucky? I don't know about that. If she'd never met me, she might be alive."

"I know it's hard to see an end when you're in the middle, but life is like a storm, right? There's always an end. And if I'd been Jen, I'd rather have known you and loved you, then to have never known you and lived a bit longer. I mean, what's the point of living if we're not alive, if we're not with people that bring us joy? To live without love isn't living in my opinion, it's only existing. Like me, just existing."

Jack rubbed his eyes again.

"I love you, Jack – I mean, not in the same way that Jen did. But I love you in my own way, and you're important to me. I'll always be your friend, Jack, no matter what happens."

Jack said, "We've gotta get out of here. We've gotta get out of Pablo's world or it's going to kill us. I'm determined to get us out. You in?"

"Yeah, I'm in."

"How do we do it?" Jack asked.

"I think I have an idea that will get us to the boat – let me figure that part out. You worry about how we get clear of these Colombian waters once we are back on *Windborne*."

31

A week had gone by since they'd decided to leave Colombia. Pablo had settled into a routine of breakfast with his father, lunch with Jack and Mariana, and family dinners with everyone together at his father's big table.

After lunch on the eighth day, Jack and Mariana decided to test their plan.

Mariana said, "Pablo, we were thinking of taking a ride this afternoon, would you like to join us?"

He looked both surprised and pleased by the request and invitation.

"I didn't know you rode, mija."

"Summer camp before high school, before I knew you, Papa."

Mariana had not referred to him so tenderly in a long time. Pablo knew that many children become rebellious. Now he believed that his patience with her had paid off. He finally had the daughter he had always wanted.

"That is a wonderful idea, mija. But today, I have a meeting with some of my father's associates and will be gone until dinner. I would love to come with you on another day."

"Well, I suppose I can forgive you this once," she said jokingly, "but I expect you to join us tomorrow." She laid her trap and easily manipulated the great manipulator. He saw only what he wanted to see.

Pablo called one of his staff over and told him to make the arrangements for their ride. Then he stood up from the table and walked the man outside of their earshot.

"Give them a nice route and ensure they are watched."

Pablo returned to the table and announced with a smile. "Your ride is all planned, and your will have a wonderful time."

The next day, butterflies could be seen dancing in rays of light and gently touching the flowers, while a chorus of birds sang out in the trees. A small herd of cattle and sheep engorged themselves on tall, green grasses, while raptors circled above searching for prey. The natural beauty of the ranch belied the ugliness of its inhabitants.

A convoy of six vehicles in total - five for security carrying twenty well-armed men - sat in the large driveway waiting for the Don and his son. Jack and Mariana walked them out and gave them a friendly wave goodbye. Mariana blew Pablo a kiss as the convoy drove off into the valley.

Then, Jack and Mariana walked over to the stable where the cabellerizo stood waiting with their saddled horses. His English was poor, so Mariana spoke to him in Spanish.

"¿Dónde deberíamos montar?"

"Hay un camino en el extremo sur del valle que te llevará hacia arriba y alrededor de la colina de allí." The man pointed as he spoke, "Es muy hermosa."

"He says we should take the trail down over there," she pointed in the same direction, "that it is very beautiful."

Jack nodded with approval. It had been a long time since he'd ridden, but the lean, fit captain deftly slipped his foot in the stirrup and threw his leg over the saddle. After Mariana was seated, they rode off down the main road towards the trail. Once they were out of earshot, Jack spoke first.

"Why not today? I mean, Pablo and his guys are gone, shouldn't we take advantage of it?"

"He's having us watched," she said definitively.

Jack looked around in all directions.

"I don't see anyone."

"He doesn't want you to see anyone, he wants you to think you're alone, and then he watches to see what you'll do. Trust me, I was a watcher."

"A watcher?"

"That's what he called us. It was one of my first jobs - he used a lot of kids, because no one pays attention to kids. He also uses some pretty advanced surveillance - I'm talking CIA-level shit."

"The trail will be watched too?" Jack asked.

"Definitely, but me asking about it would also part of the test," said Mariana.

Jack looked at her with a puzzled expression. "I don't get it."

"Pablo would reason that if we were up to no good, we wouldn't ask where to ride. His next test is to see if we take the route as laid out. The final test will be to see if we stay on the route. Tomorrow, the caballerizo will ask if we plan to take the same ride. If we say yes, two or three times, Pablo will begin to relax… I think."

"You went from very being very certain to, 'I think' – that's not real comforting."

"The wild card in all of this is that Pablo knows that I know all of this, and I already slipped away once. That's why I called him papa. That father-daughter crap is his Achilles heel. I'll be laying it on pretty thick over the next week."

"Week?"

"Yeah, no sooner. Trust me, Jack."

Jack grimaced at the thought of maintaining the charade for another week.

"If we're going to be here a week, I'm gonna make a hell of a dent in his father's tequila collection," Jack quipped.

"That's what I love about you Jack, you can always find a way to improve a bad situation with a healthy dose of booze."

They both laughed as they rode on into uncertainty.

32

By the time they were saddled up and riding on the fourth day, Jack was losing his patience.

"I don't know how much more of this I can take."

"A couple of more days, Jack. Pablo is going to ride with us tomorrow, and we'll talk about how much we love it here - play the card that you're tired of living on a boat, that kind of thing."

"Okay," he said with frustration.

"So maybe the day after tomorrow?" Jack asked impatiently.

"Yeah, we can't wait much longer because I overheard that he plans to load the boat soon and we need to get out of here before that happens."

"No shit. What time of day will we make the break?"

"Well, it was a forty-minute slow drive on the way to the ranch, how fast were we going?"

"No more than twenty."

"A horse can walk about four miles per hour. We drove for forty minutes, so how does that translate into a horse ride?"

Jack did the math quickly in his head; speed, time and distance were a captain's holy trinity.

"We drove a little over thirteen miles. That would be just over three hours on a horse walking. You can't gallop on these narrow, winding trails," he said.

"Our rides have been a little over two hours, so we are going to increase them to four," she said.

"What if we took the trail that cuts off down into that valley on the other side of the hill?" Jack asked her.

"Yeah, that might do the trick. Let's try it when he's with us tomorrow," said Mariana.

On the following day, the conversation with Pablo during their ride was actually quite enjoyable. Jack was surprised that he hadn't wanted to jump off his horse, pull Pablo to the ground, and kill him with his bare hands. The four, armed security guards who accompanied them were definitely a deterrent. Listening to Pablo talk about his youth gave Jack a different perspective on the man. *He's just like the rest of us. Broken. Fucked up.* However, despite his sympathy for Pablo, and the beauty of Colombia, Jack's moral compass was once again pointing true north. He knew the direction he had to go and wouldn't falter again. Once he had that resolve, his desire to be free of this place and these people had kicked into overdrive.

"Papa," Mariana said, "Jack and I have been wanting to take that trail off to the right, the one that goes down into the valley. How about we take it today? Please, Papa?"

"As much as I hate to say no to you, I can't do it today because I have a meeting."

"How long is the ride on that trail, Papa?"

"At least another two hours – I don't know if my ass would last that long in the saddle! I'm not a young man anymore! You should save that for another day with Jack. In fact, there is a delightful little village, and a lady that makes the best arepas and empanadas - you will have to arrive for a meal. I will have Carlos give you the instructions."

"Oooh, that sounds wonderful. Are you sure you can't join us Papa?"

"No, dear, it's really too long of a ride for me."

"Well, at least we can bring some home for you."

"Yes, that would be delightful."

Mariana's ruse was working. Pablo was so pleased that she'd wanted him along, he thought, *Maybe the time away has taught her the value of family.* He comforted himself with this revelation: She was his own prodigal child, and he would love and accept her as completely as the father in the Bible story he'd learned as a child. Mariana was about to break Pablo's heart in an irreparable way.

33

The next day, Pablo walked Jack and Mariana to the stable and had Carlos give them the instructions for the trail. He then gave them a small handwoven bag for transporting the food back to him, wished them well, and sent them on their way. They saddled up and rode out of the valley the same way they had done over the last week. Once they were out of earshot, they started to recap the plan.

"It's 10:00 o'clock now, and we'll be at the village by noon," she said.

They'd resolved that they needed to eat at the restaurant as planned before they made their break for the boat because it was likely that Pablo would have surveillance set up. After they left the restaurant, his people would call him again and she was confident that he would begin to relax and redeploy part of his team. While he didn't talk about it openly, she knew that there was some tension with other drug families, and security resources were strained. Pablo wouldn't want to tie up his team on this watch any more than absolutely necessary.

"We are fairly well provisioned on the boat, but we should buy a few items, like coffee, candy – things that wouldn't raise any suspicions," Jack said. "Maybe a few souvenirs too, like a hand-woven blanket."

"Good thinking. Once we finish in town, we'll ride back on the route that Carlos gave us until we are out of sight and on the trail. Then we can take that road that I saw intersecting the trail. We'll have to stay out of the town because he's got a lot of eyes there," Mariana noted.

"That road will cut about two hours off of our ride," Jack paused. "I can't wait to get back on *my* boat."

"We'll have about two hours before they expect us back, and that would be around 5:00 PM, right, Jack?"

"That adds up; it puts us at *Windborne* about an hour before they wonder where we are. What will be his first move?" Jack asked.

"He'll first worry that a puma or jaguar attacked us on the trail. He had a cousin killed by one when he was a boy, and he confessed to me that it's one of his only true fears. He'll probably send riders out in the direction they're expecting us to come from. That will take about an hour, and then they'll call him on a sat phone. Then he may wonder if we got lost, but even if he does, he'll check the boat –we'll be gone by then."

Jack nodded, "Yeah, gone, but not by much. We would be about fourteen miles out, but if he comes after us on a fast boat, that's maybe a half hour or less. Sunset isn't until 6:00 – he'll be onto us by 5:00 – we need another hour."

"Let's linger in the village. We can drag it out and make it look natural. Go to the market, do more shopping, drink a bottle of wine. We can make it work," she said.

"Let's have a good strong coffee too – the last thing we do – we'll need it."

The small town could have been right out of a picture book. Brightly colored alabaster walls sat beneath old, reddish, terracotta roof-tiles. Vines lazily climbed the walls, occasionally the roofs, and almost always the pergolas. Market stalls along the street sold both the necessary and unnecessary as street vendors sought to separate the meager and hard-earned income from the town folk. Occasionally, a discussion would be overheard as a price was being negotiated to the satisfaction of both parties. A fountain bubbled softly as they sat on the patio of the home, which was also the restaurant. Jack and Mariana enjoyed a peace that would soon elude them.

The lunch was everything that Pablo had described, and since they knew that they would be running hard for a few days, they ate a big meal, and let it unfold slowly. They sat and enjoyed themselves knowing it was both the beginning of their freedom, and if they were caught, the end of their lives. They savored every moment.

"Do you think there's a future for us, Jack?"

"Me and you?" Jack asked with raised eyebrows.

"Yeah, me and you." She said as she dropped her eyes away from his gaze and looked down at her lap, regretful that she'd asked a question to which she knew the answer.

"I wish there was," he reached over and lifted her chin so he could look her in the eyes. "You are everything any smart man could ever want."

"But?"

"But I've got a hole inside of me and it's still too new. I don't know when, if ever, that is going to heal."

"Well, I've got enough baggage to fill a freight train, so I'm no catch."

"I'd take all your baggage if you came with it, Mariana. Don't sell yourself short – you're the complete package. Especially for a sailin' man."

He winked at her, and it brought a smile to her face.

"Well, I guess I'll just have to content myself with being your pirate queen for a while longer, until you sail off into the sunset as most sailors eventually do."

She winked back and he smiled.

"But no matter what, we'll always be friends, right, Mariana?"

"Yeah, the same thing my senior fall prom date said to me. And I'll tell you the same thing I told him, 'You can take your friendship and...' Aww, who am I kidding, I said 'sure'."

"But we should keep the friends with benefits thing going, yeah?" Jack asked amorously.

"Oh yeah, for sure," she answered without hesitation.

They settled the bill, packed up the take-home items ostensibly for Pablo, and went in search of coffee. They found a local merchant and bought four bags, along with two hot tintos. While sipping the coffee, Mariana spoke casually with the vendor to maintain their cover. After that, they began shopping for clothes. They put on quite a performance for the watchers. Mariana would hold something up, and Jack would nod approvingly. Occasionally, he'd flash a face that indicated disapproval, but no more often than any man could reasonably expect to get away with in a relationship. Mariana was watching the watchers, and she noted on several occasions that they smiled at these exchanges between them.

Finally, when they had eaten enough and bought enough, they carefully packed up the horses and began a leisurely ride out of town on the way to the beginning of the trail. Two men in a pickup truck followed them as far as the trail, and as she glanced back carefully, she saw the satellite phone come out; Pablo would have his report, and they would have the three hours they needed to get away.

About an hour later, the boat was in sight. Jack and Mariana looked at each other and did a high-five in the air, their hands too far away to actually touch. They had carefully thought through every detail and took some sense of pride in their accomplishment.

"I can't believe we pulled this off," said Mariana.

"It's like a passage, careful planning and attention to detail," Jack said authoritatively.

"We'll be on the boat in a few minutes - anchor up and gone in twenty," he said.

One important detail had been missed.

They guided the horses along the edge of the trees until they were lined up with a group of fishing boats pulled up on the sand. They dismounted, tied off the horses, and removed the saddle bags, loading them into one of the boats closest to the water. It was when they were ready to launch the boat that Jack looked out at *Windborne* and felt his heart sink fast.

"Son of a bitch," he said in a quiet, defeated tone.

She looked up at him concerned, "What?"

He just pointed at the boat and said, "Fuck."

As she looked out at the sailboat, she saw the reason for the drop in his countenance - Pablo's man was still on the boat.

In their excitement and desire to escape Pablo, they'd completely forgotten about the man that had been left behind to keep an eye on the boat.

"What are we going to do now?" She asked him.

"I don't' know, but we better figure it out quickly. We don't have time to go back without being found out, and with that goon on the boat, we're going to have to improvise quickly," Jack said.

Time seemed to stand still as they processed what they saw. Minutes passed as they anticipated the turn of the man's head in their direction.

"I have an idea," said Jack. "Let's pray to God that the cell service sucks and that he doesn't have a sat phone."

Then Jack did the unthinkable.

"Ahoy! Ahoy there on *Windborne!"* Jack shouted at the top of his lungs.

Mariana froze in fear, having gone from a state of quiet stealth to one of extreme exposure; she felt as if she were naked. The man stood up and looked at the shore, where he saw Jack and Mariana.

"Hola. What's up? Why are you on the beach?"

As Jack expected, the guard had a lot of questions. Now, his job was to get him to stop asking them. He held up the saddlebags filled with the food and coffee.

"We brought you some things as a thank you."

Jack reached in the bag and pulled out the bottle of rum and the sack of empanadas.

"Empanadas, rum, and coffee. Bring the dinghy over. I've got a few maintenance items that are due on the boat to prepare for the next run."

He waved in acknowledgement as Jack and Mariana held their breath. Then they watched him pull out a cell phone and begin tapping the screen before putting the phone up to his ear. Tense seconds passed before he took the phone down from his head and looked at the screen.

"No service amigo," Jack whispered under his breath.

"Christ, have mercy," Mariana offered as she made the sign of the cross over her chest.

Jack and Mariana sweated anxiously as they watched him step onto the inflatable dinghy and pull the outboard starter. The engine sputtered fitfully on the first three cranks. He reached down and fiddled with what Jack could only assume was the choke. Then he took a fourth pull, and with tremendous relief, they heard the engine roar to life. He let it idle for a minute while he untied the boat, then sped off to the shore. Right before the boat hit the shallows, he killed the engine, kicked up the outboard, and let the dinghy slide up onto the sand with its own inertia. He hopped off to greet them.

"¿Quíubo caremonda? I'm surprised to see you here without Pablo or the crew." He said suspiciously.

Jack shot a quick glance at the semi-automatic pistol tucked in his waistband as he answered.

"He's been trying to call ya, it keeps going straight to voicemail," Jack lied calmly.

"Why didn't he send Jaime?"

"Got the flu – bad. They had to take him to the clinic. Pablo was worried about the whole crew getting sick, and he was worried about you because you weren't picking up. Well, he said he was worried about you, but who're we kiddin,' it's Pablo – he's worried about the boat because he needs it."

The man laughed as Jack and Mariana joined in tentatively. They were now playing a very, very, dangerous game.

"When he told us, we said we could just come by after lunch – he sent us to that restaurant in the village – San Juan. The one with the empanadas he loves, do you know it?"

"Si," he smiled and patted his belly. "The best in the region."

"Well, I told Pablo that I had to perform some maintenance to get her ready for the next run... Hey, maybe you could join us on the trip? Anyway, I suggested that after all this time on the boat, you could probably use a good meal, yeah?"

"Yes indeed, my friend."

"And, because every good sailor needs rum..." He paused and held up the bottle, "we brought you this – I hear it is the best."

In Jack's reading about Colombia, he had learned that they were very polite and hoped that his offer would necessitate reciprocity.

"Indeed, this is a very fine rum. Let's go to the boat to eat and drink together," the guard said to them.

"Oh no," Jack said dramatically, "this is for you, my friend."

"I insist!" Then he patted the gun in his waistband, "Don't make me take you at gunpoint!"

The three of them broke out into laughter.

"I'm Carlos, by the way, we didn't introduce ourselves when you arrived," he said as he extended his hand.

Jack took his hand and said, "Jack. This is the lovely Mariana," as he nodded towards her.

Jack put the bottle back in the saddle bag and handed the bags to Carlos.

As Carlos leaned over and put the bags in the dinghy, Jack's right hand drew up like a sword and came down in a flash across Carlos' neck. The sudden intense force on the brachial plexus nerve cluster created a momentary disruption in his motor functions, while the disruption in the flow of blood in his carotid artery caused a sudden spike in his blood pressure. The vagus nerve responded by sending a signal to drop the blood pressure quickly, and the man fell forward into the rubber boat – knocked out cold.

"Grab the orange case in the dinghy, there's a roll of duct tape inside. He won't be out long."

She hurriedly reached in to get the plastic case that held the dinghy's flares, whistle, VHF, and air horn.

"Here," Mariana said as her brain tried to catch up. "What do we do with him?"

"Let's get him restrained and gagged with the tape, then we can leave him in one of these fishing boats. He should be able to wiggle his way out in a few hours."

"We should probably just shoot him," she said as she pulled the gun out of his waistband.

"What the fuck, Mariana?"

"No, I mean for his own benefit, we should shoot him. Pablo or Don Julio may torture him. You never know with those two."

"No," Jack replied, "We'll leave it to fate – I don't want to kill anyone."

She nodded in agreement as they were taping Carlos' hands, feet, and mouth. Just as they were finishing, his eyes opened wide with great fright.

"Don't worry mate, we're not going to end ya," he jerked a thumb at Mariana, "she wanted to, but I said, no."

Mariana shook her head at Jack in disapproval of his humor.

"Alright, let's get on with it. Grab his feet."

Carlos struggled while Jack grabbed him under the shoulders and carried him over to one of the wooden fishing boats. They lifted him up and over the rail and heard a dull thud and groan as he hit the bottom of the boat.

"Sorry, mate," offered Jack as he turned away to get the dinghy in the water.

They took one final look around them to see if anyone was approaching or watching. Seconds later they felt the refreshing spray of the water off the bow of the dinghy as they sped across the lagoon to *Windborne.*

34

Windborne had slipped away quietly and gracefully with Jack sailing off anchor. He had put the sailboat on a beam reach at 300 degrees to get them well clear of the Islas San Bernardo before turning downwind toward Panama. The sun had set, and they'd seen no one following them. It was a new moon, and it would be a dark night; they basked in the deep blue sky fading to black.

Jack said, "I think we're in the clear. I can barely see the front of the boat. Even if they guess the right direction, they won't be able to see us until morning."

"What about their radar?"

"Sailboats of this size don't present a good target for radar - that's why we use radar reflectors. I lowered ours when we got underway."

She nodded as she took in the information.

The sailboat rode gracefully on a broad reach over a small four-foot, well-spaced swell. Jack thought, *The helm feels good without the weight of the gold, but it still doesn't feel like before the gulf storm. I wonder if it's the new quadrant and cables, maybe they've loosened and need to be adjusted.*

Mariana interrupted his train of thought, "I suspect he will think that we'll be beating up-wind to get back to Puerto Rico or the USVI – somewhere that makes it more difficult for him to harass us."

"He may just wait for us in Florida," Jack suggested.

"Which is why we can't go there – ever," she said sadly, thinking of her mom.

Jack looked at her and said, "That's the beauty of being on a sailboat when you are on the run. You may not be able to go fast, but you can go far, and the world is mostly water."

"Yeah, I'm starting to appreciate that more with every day I'm on one," she said.

"I've met sailors that have become uncomfortable on land – they'd rather be in a storm at sea than the middle of a city block."

They both sat silently for a few minutes and listened to the wind on the sails and the light splashing sound on the hull as the boat displaced the water and it rushed back in to fill the void. He had turned off all of the lights and electronics to avoid being seen from a distance.

Jack noted the direction of the predictable trade winds and steered the boat in the moonless night by keeping the wind on his right cheek and periodically glancing at the compass as they pushed out past the islands. He had missed sailing and was enjoying the dark, quiet, night. Most of all, he was enjoying his freedom. Occasionally, he'd pull out his phone and look at the navigation app to make sure he wasn't being pushed too far west before they cleared the islands. Soon he'd engage the wind vane and let mechanics and physics do the work for him.

Jack broke the silence in a commanding tone of voice and said, "I've made a lot of shitty compromises and broke a ton of laws over the last few months, now it's time to break one of my rules."

"Yeah, what's that – not having sex at sea with your first mate?"

Jack paused before he answered. "Hmmm, I hadn't considered that possibility. Ok, I'll break two rules."

"What's the first?"

"Go get us a slug of that rum," he smiled at her.

"Aye-aye Cap'n."

She disappeared below into the dark as Jack took another deep breath. He sat there in those moments and considered everything that had led up to that point. The Gulf Stream, the drunken mess that followed, the Coast Guard review board, that fateful call from Pablo, and meeting Mariana. Now here he was with her, both of them trying to escape from different pasts and the same man, like fugitives of the divine. Jack thought to himself as he pondered questions of their fate, *Maybe she was right. Maybe this is all by the design of the universe, God, or a program in a simulation. How can a series of seemingly unconnected events connect so perfectly if it's not by design?* With a final, very deep breath, he sighed and let the weight come off him. He knew it would return, but at least he could free himself from its claw-like grip for an evening. He'd drink rum in his favorite mug, enjoy Mariana's company, and make love to her on the deck of his sailboat. Jack reasoned that in this life, even one night such as this makes a life worth living.

35

Don Julio was furious with his son's indiscretion. Even as an old man, his bear-like hand easily knocked Pablo to the floor as it raked across his face. Pablo still trembled like a child in the fury of his father's wrath. He pulled himself to his feet as the servants and crew averted their gaze to avoid this awkward family moment.

"You stupid, emotional fool! Did I not teach you this lesson a hundred times! You cannot let your emotions govern your decisions! They should have been chaperoned! What were you thinking? No, clearly you were not thinking. Is it her cuca? Is that what is twisting up your mind? Are you hard for her? Or maybe Jack? Quizás, Pablo sea un maricon. Why do you treat this Capitan with such great reverence? We could buy and sell a hundred men such as him. What do you have to say for yourself?"

Pablo began to speak but his father cut him off, "No, never mind. I don't want to hear your weak excuses; it may cause me to vomit. America has weakened you, and clearly, I've trusted you with far too much. Trust, I thought you had earned. This is my fault - I should have known that after all these years you are just a boy, not a man. You will never be a man."

The room remained silent as Pablo's father paced the floor, considering his next move, which unbeknownst to Pablo, included whether or not he should call for the execution of his own son.

He turned to his security team and said, "Find them, kill them and bring me their heads – ten thousand dollars for each will be given to you when you lay their heads on THIS TABLE!" He pounded the table so hard with his massive fist, that the table settings rattled, and a glass of wine toppled over."

"Father, not her. You may kill him, but you may not kill her, she is a daughter to me, and I've given her our family crest."

Looks of shock flashed across the faces of every man and woman in the room. They stood in disbelief that Pablo had challenged the great Don - and did so in his own home. It was an insult that would not go unanswered. Before the shock could leave their faces, the big man pulled a gun from his waistband and pointed it at his son's head.

"You should die for this… You know that. You have compromised our family, my business, our fortunes, and for what? Did you even wet your shrimp dick in her pussy? Or perhaps you do prefer men - you've never married. Is that why you like Jack so much?"

The insult stung him deeply. All of his life, Pablo had heard his father using words like maricon and sissy to berate those he despised - those he thought weak. It was another way that the big man stepped on people as hate spewed from his mouth.

In that moment, all Pablo could feel was that his foundation had been smashed out from under him as he stared into the barrel of a gun.

Don Julio looked around the room to see if anyone would offer an opinion. Then, without warning, he shifted his aim away from Pablo and pulled the trigger. The servants and security guards looked on in horror as the head of a houseboy exploded onto the wall, and he fell to the floor in a messy heap. He had decided that someone needed to die, but he wasn't yet ready to kill his own son.

The big man screamed at the top of his lungs, "Now, go and find those fucking traitors! Kill them and brink me back my cocaine! Somebody clean up this goddamn mess before dinner!"

He took one last look at Pablo, shook his head, sighed in disappointment, and walked out of the room. Pablo stood without moving for several more minutes. He was weary of being treated like a little boy.

36

The rum was good, the sex was better. After they had satisfied each other, Jack had turned *Windborne* west-southwest toward Panama and engaged the wind vane steering system. He had dozed off a few times in the cockpit before Mariana woke him and sent him below. Now, she dutifully stood watch under a starless sky while she let the man she loved sleep in peace. Laying on her back looking up at the cloud cover, desperately trying to pierce it with her vision and find some light.

Her thoughts were filled with what would come next and she wasn't hopeful about the prospects. There was a sick feeling in her stomach that Pablo would see this as the final betrayal, and he would have his vengeance. It was then that she started to plan her final escape. This time she would make sure that she would be forever free of the man who had used her and corrupted her youth by preying on her vulnerabilities. She refused to live any longer in a world in which fear was the sunrise and despair the sunset.

Time for a glass of water and a pee. She stood up to go below and then froze in her footsteps as she looked off the back of the boat. Her eyes were straining in the night.

"Dear God, don't let that be what I think it is."

There it was again, there was a light appearing and disappearing over the edge of the horizon.

"Oh fuck!" Mariana said loudly as she turned and practically jumped below holding on to the ladder rails tightly and sliding down them as her long legs found the moving cabin sole beneath her feet. She made her way quickly to Jack's berth and flung open the door.

"Jack, Jack, wake up. I saw a boat's steaming light."

A foggy minded Jack Kelly tried to interpret what his ears had just heard as his subconscious processed the information while dumping adrenaline into his body. He bolted upright in his bed.

"What the… A light? Are you sure?" Jack asked.

"Yeah, white light. Bouncing in and out of view at the edge of the horizon. How far is that?"

"Depends on their height above the water, but assuming the worst, about six miles," he answered.

"How long do we have before they get here?" Mariana asked him with desperation.

"That depends on their speed – how's the swell?"

"Heavier, hard to tell in the dark, but maybe six to eight feet," she said.

"That'll help, and obviously it depends on the boat too. I'd say best case, forty minutes; worst case, twenty," the Captain said definitively. "Everything is still off, right? No AIS, yeah?"

"Right, nothing is on. If it's them - and we need to assume it is - how the hell did they find us on a pitch-black night, Jack?"

He rubbed his eyes and thought deeply about her question. He opened his mouth to say something, and then stopped and put both hands over his mouth in a praying motion, then he dropped them hard on his thighs. Jack started shaking his head as if in denial of what his mouth was about to say, "There's got to be a tracker on board. Turn on the lights and start looking for it. I'd check those compartments that Pablo used for the gold. He probably left them knowing that we'd be doing another run."

She felt her stomach sink. *Pablo. Always fucking Pablo.* She hadn't known anything else since she was a kid. If it hadn't been for her loyalty to Jack, she would have walked to the back of the boat and stepped off into the dark, Colombian waters. Jack could see her drifting into despair and interrupted her fantasy about suicide by putting her to work.

"Shake it off and focus! Start looking!" He put his hands on her shoulders as he stood up. "We'll figure it out, I promise."

He knew it was a promise he might not be able to keep, but nevertheless, one that had to be made.

"Aye, Cap," she said dutifully.

Mariana turned toward the electrical panel and flipped on the main cabin power switch. A few more switches were flipped at various locations and the darkness was vanquished. She began moving cushions, opening lockers, and looking under the cabin sole boards underneath her feet. It only took a few seconds before she found what they sought along with a shocking discovery.

"Jack! Oh my God. The boat is loaded with cocaine!" she said as she leaned over and picked up a tracking device. "Yep, here it is."

She held it up as Jack walked over to look at the drugs in the bilge area.

"What the fuck? I swear I'll kill that son of a bitch if I ever see him again," he said with hate and fierce determination.

They stood silently, both contemplating what would follow. Then, Jack turned and started doing something that seemed wholly inappropriate to the execrable moment they were now experiencing. She stared at him speechless in complete disbelief.

"Jesus in heaven, Jack, are you making coffee?"

The Captain smiled and turned to look at her. She noticed that his face was as calm as a windless day, and he had a determined look in his eyes.

"Well Mariana, it is very good coffee; and I would like to sit down, relax and have a cup while we finish sorting this out."

She wanted to slap him because she needed him to be as fearful as she was at that moment; but she looked into his eyes and could see that her captain had a plan. So, instead of arguing, she took a deep breath and let it out slowly.

"Would ya make one for me too?"

"It would be my pleasure," said the Captain as he turned back to the galley stove.

Jack filled a kettle with water, flicked on the solenoid that allowed the propane to flow from the tanks to the stove, and turned on the burner. As if he hadn't a care in the world, he moved slowly and deliberately, placing the kettle carefully between the two holders that kept it from sliding around, and then slowly ground the beans. With a smile on his face, he began humming the sea shanty *Captain Kidd.* When he finished loading the French press, he turned toward her and leaned back, bracing himself casually against the galley counter. Crossing his arms and cocking his head, in a rather smug tone, he asked, "Mariana, my dear, have you done much reading on British naval history around the Napoleonic wars?"

"I have not."

"Wonderful, wonderful. Tonight, I am going to introduce you to one of Britain's finest naval commanders. Flip on the sailing lights, I want our friends to get a good look at us."

37

The men in the boat could finally see it – a faint light appearing and disappearing became ever so slightly more visible as they moved toward it.

"That's them! We've got them! Call Pablo!"

Miguel pulled out a satellite phone, powered it up, and opened the antenna. He stared at the screen while it acquired the satellites, and waited for the symbol to indicate there was a good signal. Once he had it, he pulled up Pablo's contact information and made the call.

Over the roar of the motor and the movement of water on the hull, he yelled into the phone, "Boss, we've got them. The GPS tracker led us right to them."

Pablo's face showed a mixture of relief mixed with concern, "That is good," he said with as much enthusiasm as he could muster. "I will tell the Don. How long?"

"Thirty minutes or so."

"Bueno. Call me again when the load is secure."

Pablo hung up the phone and set it down on the table. He knew what he had to do next. As with many things in his life it would be something he considered unpleasant, yet necessary.

While the men in the boat sped toward *Windborne,* Pablo walked down the hall to his father's study to make one final attempt to reason with an unreasonable man. He was not hopeful about the outcome of the conversation.

38

"Have you ever head of Admiral Lord Cochrane?" Jack asked her as he walked over to the library.

"No," she answered in a tone revealing curiosity.

He pulled an old hardcover book off the shelf titled *The Autobiography of a Seaman,* set it down on the table, and then thumbed through its well-worn pages until he found the passage he was looking for.

"Listen to what he did one night while being chased, '*Before they had fairly renewed the chase, night was rapidly setting in, and when quite dark, we lowered a ballasted cask overboard with a lantern, to induce them to believe that we had altered course, though we held on in the same direction during the whole night. The trick was successful, for, as had been calculated, the next morning, to our great satisfaction, we saw nothing of them...'* Quite something, isn't it!"

"Wasn't that in the movie, *Master and Commander?"*

"Indeed, it was, my dear - one of my favorites! Well, the exploits of that fictional captain were at least partially based on Cochrane's career," he said, pointing to the book. "And now *this* Captain," he said as he jerked a thumb back at himself, “is going to use the same trick as Cochrane!”

She could tell that Jack was quite pleased with himself. However, now ten minutes into the chase, she was getting worried that he tarried too long in the delight of his game.

“We’re going to lower some lanterns onto the dinghy?” Mariana asked him impatiently.

“No, my dear girl. We are going to do the modern-day equivalent.”

39

Pablo appeared in the study, and he could tell by the look on his father's face that he was disgusted with him. It seemed the Don could barely tolerate his presence. Before he could speak, Don Julio turned away from him and sat down in a chair facing the fireplace.

"Good news, Don Julio," he knew better than to call him father at a time like this. "The men called, and they have found the boat; they will overtake it in about thirty minutes."

Don Julio nodded in approval.

"We will have our cocaine back, and you will have your satisfaction. Now, I must speak with you about the matter of Mariana and Jack. We must not kill them," he said arrogantly.

His father's head spun around so quickly that it looked like it should have snapped his neck. "You dare to question my decision just hours after I spared your life?"

"You would never kill me, Don. Not because you love me – oh, I know that you do not love me - for *you* have never loved anyone. No, you won't kill me because you are a smart businessman. Think of all the gold that I will move here. You would never risk all of that gold, would you, Papa?" Pablo said 'papa' in a mocking tone.

The Don stood up slowly and glared at him.

"Well, perhaps I underestimated your cunning, young Pablo," he nodded in affirmation as he considered his own words. "Perhaps. But this is neither here nor there, my decision about Jack and Mariana is final. You may not like it, but you *will* carry out my orders!"

"Or what?" Pablo said defiantly as he now turned away from the old man and went to the liquor cart to pour himself a glass of scotch.

His father was enraged by the impudence. "Or what? Have you lost your mind? Have you forgotten who I am?"

"How could any of us forget who you are? You are the great Don Julio; all people bend to your will - or so you would have us believe. None of us are permitted to choose our path based on our own desires," said Pablo in an air of contempt.

"You little pig of a man! First you question me, and now you insult me in my own home?"

"A pig of a man comes from a hog of a father."

"You fool!" Don Julio shouted. "Do you think you are above my authority? Do you really believe that I would not kill you?"

"Yes, I do think I'm above your authority and no, as I have already said, you will not kill me, because you want the gold. And you certainly care about that metal more than you do your *satisfaction,* don't you? You disgusting old beast!"

Don Julio had heard enough. He looked at the big pistol on the fireplace mantel that he had just used to kill the servant. He thought he was done killing for the night, but he now knew that he had been wrong. Pablo saw him glance at the pistol and waited for him to reach for it, at this point, he truly didn't care whether or not his father killed him. He was tired of this endless loop of attempting to please the unpleasable.

But to Pablo's surprise, his father didn't reach toward the gun. He stopped and looked at his son again. When he finally spoke, it was slowly and with regret, "Perhaps I have failed you as a father."

Pablo was shocked at the statement, and suddenly hopeful. But then the great Don did what he always did, he found a way to elevate himself at the expense of all others.

"Or perhaps you are not *my* son."

Pablo looked up shocked. The old man could see that once again, he had found the part of Pablo that he could control.

"Perhaps, it was your whore of a mother. Yes, that must be the source of this foolish behavior, it was the seed of some other fool that made you the fool that you are. You certainly couldn't be mine..." He trailed off, his tone littered with disappointment.

But Pablo did not cower or retreat, he boldly said, "Don Julio, you must think me an idiot to believe such a magnificent tale! To think that you, the great Don, would allow your wife to have sex with other men? Why would she need to?" He paused for a moment to set up the hateful blow. "Perhaps you are right... Perhaps she slept with other men because you couldn't get it up? Ha! That explains the bravado and big guns - your own dick doesn't work!"

The big man's eyes grew wide as his pupils dilated from the rise in his anger and adrenaline pumping through his bloodstream. He had heard all that he could hear. He knew that his son must die tonight, and tomorrow he would bury him next to his mother. He started to move towards the gun when he heard the slide of a semi-automatic pistol racking a round into the chamber; it was a sound he knew well. The Don froze in his tracks and slowly turned to face his son.

"Remember this gun, Papa?"

His father nodded.

"I remember the day you gave it to me. I was so proud. I was even happy to kill for you – did you know that? But you were never proud of me, were you? I was never man enough for you, was I, Papa? Never macho enough..."

His father remained silent. For the first time in many decades, he faced the working end of a gun. He had forgotten what it felt like.

Pablo continued, "I tried so hard, so hard! I tried to do the impossible - to make you happy and earn your respect!"

The two men locked their gaze and stood silently before Pablo continued.

"But nothing was ever enough, was it? I killed that boy at school on my birthday, then the man at the fountain, then the young girl at the coffee shop, then your own cousin!"

Pablo shook his head in disgust at himself and his father.

"I have killed so many that I can't even remember them all. Do you know that sometimes I try? I lay awake at night trying to remember their names, or the reason why they had to die, and mostly it's all faded from my mind. It's all like a dark mist. There's your legacy, old man. Lives destroyed for your debased and selfish purposes."

The big man remained silent, his left eye was twitching as Pablo began to pace the floor, occasionally tapping the gun to his head.

"What was it that you taught me, Papa?" Pablo had determined he would never again call the man 'Don.' "You taught me not to leave anyone alive that could come back and kill you. Well, you should be proud of your accomplishments as a teacher, because I was paying attention to every word, every move, and every deed." He tapped his head again with the pistol. "I have them all up here, like a tape recording that I watch over and over and over."

Pablo laughed in an evil tone, "Hahaha. Yes, Papa, I learned from you all that I know. That is your legacy, your great legacy. It's not the land, or the pallets of U.S. dollars, or the gold. It's the hatred, the evil… the destruction."

His father started to speak, "Son-" but Pablo cut him off.

"Don't you dare to call me, son. No, I am Pablo to you, *DON* Pablo."

His father's face contorted when he heard his son refer to himself as the Don. Then, he began to sweat and struggle with his breath. He could feel a shooting pain in his arm as his chest began to tighten.

"Well, old man, I have decided that Mariana *and* Jack will live. Maybe I am a sentimental fool, but it's got to be better than ending up a lonely old man surrounded by people who are afraid of him. I no longer want to be you, old man, I no longer want to be you!"

His father started to sit down, and then collapsed into the chair as he gasped for air and clutched his heart.

Without a hint of concern, Pablo said, "What's wrong, is the old ticker giving out on you?"

His father was unable to answer.

"Not the way you planned to go, eh, old man?"

His father shook his head.

"Good, that's not what I planned either. I want you to know that you lost. You lost to your best student, and you lived long enough to see how the tables have turned. Not to die by some unexpected heart attack! But I want you to leave this world with a full understanding of who your son really is – the son you never had a chance to know. Not only am I better than you… I'm gay - you bigoted son of a bitch."

His father's eyes grew wide with shock and disbelief. He managed to utter only one word, "Maricon." Even with his dying breath, all the man could do was hate.

Pablo shook his head in sorrow, "You will never understand who I am. You will die having never known your own son…" Pablo's voice trailed off.

He could feel his anger leaving him after finally telling his father the truth. Pablo was left with nothing but pity for the man, and the resolve to save himself, Jack, and Mariana.

He leveled the gun and emptied the magazine into his father, putting all the rounds into his chest but away from his heart. He wanted the old man to feel every bullet and understand what it must have felt like for all the people that he had killed.

When the pistol was empty, he deftly dropped the magazine and reloaded. Expecting a security guard to burst into the room, he let the slide release to chamber a round, and turned to face the door, which burst open as if on cue. Riot shotguns at the ready, the two men froze as they entered the room to see that Pablo had the drop on them.

"This old man was a son of a bitch, and you know it. He had no loyalty to you or anyone but himself. You saw the way he killed that servant boy to satisfy his own rage."

The men nodded.

"You work for me now. I am tough, but I am fair, and I won't kill you unless you betray me or steal from me."

The men thought of the gold that he had given each of them when he had arrived. Pablo was many things, but he was no fool; he had foreseen the many possibilities. He knew that he could buy them the same way his father had. Now that their meal ticket was dead, they needed a new one. It was as simple as that; he knew that poverty enables lawlessness and money advances loyalty.

After the men left the room, Pablo gazed upon the lifeless form of the ego that had dominated his life. He finally felt a sense of complete freedom.

"Maria!" Pablo shouted loud enough to be heard through the house as his voice reverberated off of the hard adobe walls and tiled floors.

He sat down in the chair opposing his dead father and waited patiently with the pistol in his lap. Seconds later, Maria flung open the door to the study and saw the unusual scene before her. Pablo sat in a chair next to his dead father, as if they were casually conversing in front of the fire.

"¿Sí, señor?" She stood frozen, the color draining out of her face.

He answered her in Spanish.

"Maria, my father has resigned as the head of the family, and I have taken his place. I need you to do three things in this order: Bring me two glasses of my father's favorite tequila – one for me, and one for him. After we have finished our drinks, prepare his body for burial, and call the priest. When you have finished cleaning up, assemble the staff. Obviously that chair will have to be burned with the garbage – actually, burn both of them; I never liked them." A smile came across his face, and he said, "We will have new ones made with fine leather. Won't that be nice?"

"Sí, Don. Muy bueno."

She bowed slightly as she left the room. When she reentered the room, Pablo was so engrossed in his thoughts he had not even noticed the tequila that she had set before him.

Don Pablo sat and considered his plans for retrieving the rest of the gold from America. Now that he was the head of the family, it would not be practical for him to risk another trip to the States. He realized that he would need Jack and Mariana even more than he had anticipated and he would have to find their price. He considered the situation. *They want each other, but is that enough? Both of them clearly want to escape, but freedom is the one thing that I can't offer.* He paused his thoughts for a minute before continuing. *It doesn't matter, they will return if they want their lives spared - that's what I'll offer them.*

Pablo stood up, picked up the first glass of tequila and raised it toward the dead body. Then, without a word, tossed it in the fire where it flashed in the flame, gone as quickly as the life he had just taken.

Pablo turned toward the dead man and said contemplatively, "This has turned into such a wonderful day... Isn't it interesting father? If Jack and Mariana had not fled, you and I wouldn't have had this conversation and disagreement. This is the great mystery of life, how God watches over all of us and directs our path. He made you to watch over me and raise me up for this great and glorious day – I will be much better than you, and God knew this."

With all of that settled, he lifted his own glass of tequila and drank it in one shot. Pablo threw the glass hard into the fireplace, shattering it into pieces. Then, he walked to his room, picked up the phone and dialed the boat.

"How long?" Don Pablo impatiently asked Miguel.

"The swell is a little steeper now, and we had to slow down... about twenty minutes," he answered.

"Bien. Listen carefully to me. Jack and Mariana will live, I will explain it all later. If anyone harms them, they will be executed. Make sure your men know this."

Pablo hung up the phone and went back to *his* study. He continued to reflect upon the changes he would make to build upon his father's empire. The child inside of him still felt that while his father would disagree with the new direction, he would surely be proud if he were alive to see it.

40

As Jack had unfolded his plan, the smile on Mariana's face had grown wider by the minute.

"Does that make sense?" He asked her.

"Yep. I'll gather the stuff we need."

Jack had been monitoring the other boat's progress on his own radar and noticed that it had slowed down over the last few minutes. The barometer was dropping. It felt like a squall line was approaching, and even though storms had not been kind to the Captain, he welcomed this one. The cover and concealment from the rain and clouds would further darken the sky and work in his favor.

The sailing lights which Jack had asked Mariana to turn on were located on top of the fifty-foot-tall mast. He had wanted to ensure that his pursuers could clearly see *Windborne.* It wasn't essential to the plan, but Jack wanted the satisfaction of shutting off the lights as Cochrane had done, centuries before him. The ruse played out in his mind, first Cochrane's and then his own. A smug smile decorated his face while he thought about the reaction Pablo would have when he found out.

A few minutes later, Mariana appeared with the items in her hands and dropped them on the table. Before them sat a small dry bag, sandwich bags, a roll of duct tape, a life jacket, and the three GPS trackers that they had found on the boat.

Jack triple bagged the trackers in resealable plastic sandwich bags before he put them in the dry bag. Then he tightened the straps on the lifejacket, so the floats were pulled together tightly. Finally, he strapped the dry bag to the lifejacket and duct taped the whole bundle together.

“Showtime Lieutenant,” Jack said in an English accent.

“Lieutenant?” Mariana questioned.

“Yeah, the first officer would have likely been a lieutenant - now stay in character or you’re going to spoil the damn fun!”

Mariana laughed and smiled. She was amazed by a man that could be so calm, as a boat of armed men bore down on them in a ten-foot swell. But like all good captains, Jack knew that a calm and cheerful demeanor was essential to the boat’s morale. He’d already had his moment of failure and despair in the Gulf Stream, where he’d been tested and broken. Now Jack had the confidence of a true sea captain, and the wisdom from his experiences. He was now the man that would win back his life and his license.

“Lieutenant, take this package, deploy one of the life rafts. Once the raft has inflated, place the package inside,” he said as he handed her the package. "We shall christen her the HMS Cochrane," Jack said with a broad smile. "Then untie the painter line and let the raft go adrift. Once she's a few boat lengths behind us, scream, *lights!* At that moment, I'll flip off the lights. Then we'll disengage the wind vane and I'll take the helm. We'll sail right back at 'em - and on this dark, stormy night, we could pass within a half mile, and they'd never even know we were there."

Mariana said with a smile, "You've gotta love sailboats."

Jack winked and smiled back at her.

"Shouldn't we toss the drugs, too?" Mariana asked him.

"No, because if this doesn't work, we might need them to cut a deal," he said.

Mariana did as she was instructed, first deploying the raft, then pulling it close enough to load the lifejacket. It was challenging in the swell, but she had harnessed up and clipped in. Once the package was on the raft, she released the painter line and watched as the boat disappeared quickly in the dark water behind them.

"LIGHTS!" Mariana screamed at the top of her lungs. Then she disengaged the wind vane and held the boat on course.

Jack flipped off the navigation lights, the cabin lights and all of the electronics before going on deck. The Captain would now pilot his boat by hand and feel on the pitch-black night - right back toward the men that chased him.

Jack took his place behind the helm and turned the boat upwind as he called out instructions for the sail trim.

"Trim for close hauled, we'll point right back toward those sons of bitches, and they'll know what true seamanship is when they find that raft!" He laughed loudly over the growing wind. "Once we're past them, we'll take a reef – feels like a squall is building in."

Mariana nodded in response.

Jack turned the boat and set the helm on the new course by the feeling of the wind on his right cheek and nose. Mariana trimmed the genoa first and then the main sail as Jack had taught her. She couldn't see the telltales, so she listened to the sails to see if they were luffing and noisy. As she felt the boat accelerating onto the new heading, she could tell that *Windborne* was happy. So was its master.

Mariana had never seen Jack this happy before. His skill and cleverness had allayed her fears. This moment of inner peace gave her the clear head she needed to contemplate her own next steps. She realized that the loose ends would have to be tied up if she was ever to find lasting peace.

41

The men on the chase boat noticed something was wrong within a few minutes of the events on *Windborne.* The man in charge spoke first.

"Look at this," Miguel pointed to the tablet, "the trackers have slowed down and are moving very slowly west. What do you make of this?"

The men looked at each other in a puzzled manner and offered no response.

Miguel spoke again, "What if they found the drugs and they've stopped to dump the cargo? God forbid, I don't want to return empty handed on this night. Don Julio would kill us!" he said, for he had not yet learned about the fate of his employer. "Push it as hard as you can – we have to get there quickly!"

The man at the helm, Captain "Big" Jim, reached down and pushed the twin throttles forward on the fifty-nine-foot flybridge cruiser. Its twin, six-hundred horsepower engines moved the boat ahead faster, and the captain carefully steered the boat in the increasing swell.

"That's it, no faster in this swell. We'll be there in ten to fifteen minutes," said Big Jim.

42

Jack and Mariana stood on deck watching the lights of the power boat as it continued on its course. Their ruse had worked; the powerboat was headed straight to where they had left the HMS Cochrane. With both boats heading towards each other at an angle, the distance between them closed quickly, and they watched in satisfaction as it passed by them not more than five hundred yards away. Jack raised the handheld FLIR night vision scope and was able to get a good look at the boat; he could make out four people on the flybridge.

"Take a look," Jack said, handing her the scope.

Mariana tried to steady herself against the binnacle while she sighted the fast-moving boat. Using any kind of monocular or binocular was not an easy task in a rough sea, and at the moment, *Windborne* was bashing upwind in a ten-foot swell, making it nearly impossible.

"Ha! That'll teach them not to chase a real sailing captain, eh?" He turned to high-five her. "Well done, Lieutenant, well done!"

She bowed theatrically, and then comically almost fell over as a wave crossed under the boat at an unusual angle.

"Steady. Steady now, mate!" Jack said in his English accent. "A tot of rum for the crew and captain if you please, Miss Hansen."

Mariana played along, answering him in a Cockney accent, "Righ' away, Cap'n!"

Mariana went below to find the rum and cups. It was not easy to find her way around in the pitch-black boat saloon, but she had been on *Windborne* long enough to know where everything was. Within a few minutes she was back on deck with the two steel mugs of rum. She handed one to Jack and sat down next to the helm.

"Cheers!" Mariana said enthusiastically as she raised the mug.

"Long live the King," Jack said.

"Long live the King," she echoed with vigor… Wait, I thought they have a queen?"

"Well, our characters are in the timeframe of the Napoleonic Wars – so that would have been King George III," Jack said in a scholarly fashion.

She nodded at his admonishment, and asked, "What now, Cap?"

"Let's crack off a little to a beam reach and get these swells on our side, it'll stop this incessant bashing. We'll sail off and make some northing for a while before we make our next turn and run west. If they look for us, my sense is they will head straight downwind."

"Where are we headed?" Mariana asked.

"Let's stick with Panama. I sure as hell don't want to take Cape Horn to starboard – I've read that book. After that, I'm headed to the Marquesas. You're welcome to come along."

"I'd love to go with you… Aren't you worried that Pablo will look for us in Panama?"

"Yeah, he would. But that's why I held onto the cocaine, I've got another plan cookin'," Jack said as he drained the mug and tapped the empty cup to his head.

"Of course you do, Jack Kelly."

She smiled at him tenderly and wished that they could love each other completely. *If only we were unpolluted and could spend the rest of our lives sailing Windborne…* However, she knew that neither the boat nor the man could ever truly be hers, for both belonged to another.

"Ok, Polynesia it is. But I need to take a week off while we're in Panama. I've gotta take care of a few things with my family before we go. Cool?"

"Yeah, we can lay up there for a bit on the west coast – there's a good marina that my friend Simon told me about. It's a few hours north of Panama City, Vista Mar Marina. It should be far enough off the beaten path to keep us safe while we prepare for the passage. Apparently, they've got a good staff and facilities. Plus, there's markets nearby where we can provision for the passage. The timing's not right to leave yet anyway, we've gotta wait a bit for the trades to fill in."

"Can I keep my rank of lieutenant?" Mariana asked jokingly.

"Well, it's a temporary battle promotion, my dear, and of course it will need to be confirmed by the admiralty. And, you'll have to submit your logs and go through your examinations – there can be no show of favoritism!" He said this sternly, as a Master and Commander would to a young officer in His Majesty's Navy.

"Thank ye kindly, sir!"

They laughed and enjoyed a moment that they had never imagined possible as they played out their little HMS *Windborne* skit. For the moment, Jack and Mariana were at peace. They desperately needed these moments.

For *Windborne's* part, she drove north forcefully with the swell on her beam, as if she too knew that they were on the run.

43

The yacht that had chased *Windborne* tirelessly now idled slowly in the large swell, moving just fast enough to maintain helm control and an optimal angle to the following seas. The night was now black and wet as rain dumped on them. Eerie spotlights swept the water as two men stood out on the bow with handheld searchlights looking for any sign of the sailboat.

"Maybe it went down," one man shouted to the other.

"This storm is not that bad," said the second man.

The GPS indicated that they should be right on top of the boat, so they started looking for anything.

"I just saw a reflection!" Big Jim called to them over the loudspeaker. "Move your light back to your left, Jesus."

Jesus did as instructed and slowly panned the light to his left.

"There!"

"Jesus, keep the light on that raft."

"Pedro, grab a long boat hook."

Big Jim saw the orange and reflective tape clearly now, and he maneuvered the yacht to come along side and upwind of the raft, blocking the wind and swell as they brought it aboard with a hoist used for jet skis.

"Do you think they put the cocaine in the raft and left?" Miguel asked desperately.

"I sure as hell hope so," Captain Jim answered.

"Even with the cocaine, we are coming back without Jack and Mariana," Miguel said in defeat. He knew that they had been bested, and he understood the repercussions.

After the raft was on board, one of the men opened the storm cover while the other stood with his weapon at the ready in case someone was inside. It was a very anticlimactic moment when they found only the PFD and package that Jack had left for them. He pulled it out quickly and walked it over to Miguel.

"This is it, Jefe. No cocaine."

Miguel tried to remain composed as he examined the package carefully. Then, he pulled out a pocketknife and cut it open to find the tracking devices in plastic bags, and a handwritten note that Jack had slipped in without Mariana's knowledge. Miguel read the note which said:

Pablo,
Not today.
Cheers,
Captain Jack

Miguel wanted to wad the note up and throw it in the sea. He dreaded the thought of coming back empty handed. He knew that it would not bode well for his future with the organization or even the continuation of his life.

He handed the note to the Captain because he wanted someone else to share in the misery of the moment. Big Jim read the note and handed it back to Miguel.

"Not good, buddy. Not good at all."

"He's going to kill us."

"Hey, speak for yourself, I'm a skilled captain – no offense, but I'm harder to replace than a gunslinger."

Miguel smirked at him. He knew the captain wasn't wrong. Don Pablo loved Captain Jim. Pablo even invited Jim to join him for dinner and drinks when they traveled together to Cuba. He was the only member of Pablo's staff treated with such respect and courtesy.

"Might as well get this over with," Miguel said as he opened the satellite phone and punched the number on the auto dial.

Pablo heard the phone ringing and went down the hallway to answer it. He was certain that it would be good news; he expected to hear that his drugs, his captain, and his daughter were safe and on their way home. Everything would come together as he had carefully planned.

"Hola," Pablo said as he picked up the phone.

"Boss, no good news here. We found the trackers in a dry bag taped to a PFD. They could have just thrown them overboard – they obviously wanted us to find them."

"So, they led you off course. Those two are clever and crafty," Pablo said with admiration.

"Yeah, I think they wanted us to follow the trackers, which explains why we lost sight of the masthead light at around the same time we thought the boat had slowed down."

"Well done, Jack. Well done, indeed," Pablo said.

Miguel was surprised that Pablo was not screaming; he was glad, but it also worried him.

"Don Julio will be furious, Pablo. I know that I am a dead man – he will surely have me killed. Please take care of my children."

"He will not kill you, Miguel."

"Why not?"

"A dead man cannot pull a trigger."

"What? Don Julio is dead? What happened?"

"I emptied my forty-five into his chest."

The phone remained silent for a few seconds.

"You will not have me killed?"

"Of course not, Miguel! You are a loyal man – and I need loyal men. Do not ever lie to me or steal from me."

"Never, Don Pablo. Never!"

It brought Pablo great satisfaction to hear him being called, "Don" by one of his father's soldiers.

"Was there anything else other than the trackers?" Pablo asked.

Miguel wished he hadn't shown the note to Jim and had instead just thrown it in the black ocean.

"There was a note from Jack," said Miguel with hesitation.

"Well, what did it say?"

"All it said was, 'Not today.'"

"Was it addressed to me or my father?"

"To you, Don."

Pablo sighed deeply. *That smug son of a bitch.* This was a tremendous disappointment, but Pablo was determined to maintain a cooler head than his father.

"Very well. Go wait for him in Panama, I'm sure that was his destination. He talked of Polynesia often, and that would be the gateway to the Pacific."

Pablo set the phone down and went back to the study. He saw that it was being cleaned as he had instructed, so he went to the living room, where a large oil painting of Don Julio hung above the fireplace and greeted him with a stern look as he entered the room.

"Maria!" Pablo shouted.

The middle-aged woman who served as the head of the maid staff appeared quickly.

"¿Sí, señor?"

He said in Spanish, "Burn this painting of my father and call an artist to have one done of me."

"Sí, Don, lo entiendo," Maria said to indicate that she understood the instructions, and then left the room abruptly.

The new Don went over to the tequila tray, poured a well-aged añejo tequila, and sat down on the soft brown leather couch. He thought back to his childhood, recalling a game that he and his father had played on the same couch. Pablo recalled how in those brief moments, he was not terrified of the big man. For once, it had felt so good to laugh and play as a young boy. Sadly, the moment had been interrupted by unwelcome news from one of his crew, and his father left the room. A week had gone by before young Pablo worked up enough courage to ask his father to play another game. He was rewarded for his courage by a hard, back-handed strike across his mouth that caused his eyes to well up in tears immediately.

"Stop with your foolish childhood games and go do some work!" Don Julio had shouted furiously at the eight-year-old boy.

So the young Pablo found a way to make money by teaching some of the servants to read in their off-work hours. His father never complimented him directly, but one day, when his father saw that Pablo had a particularly large handful of coins, he received an approving nod from the man that he worshipped. He had continued from that day to work hard for his father's approval.

He drained the glass, poured another, and thought, *Now, I will work hard for myself.*

44

Mariana woke Jack for his upcoming watch. He'd had four solid hours of sleep but was still a bit groggy. During the night, she had made the course change as Jack had instructed - west-southwest back towards Panama. They were well over the horizon, or "two horizons" as Jack liked to say, about twelve nautical miles from where they passed the yacht chasing them before she jibed the boat and brought them back onto a broad reach. The squall had blown through quickly and the waves were already lessening.

Jack rubbed his eyes, slid out of the berth, and walked into the galley. He leaned against the counter to brace himself and she pushed a fresh cup of coffee at him which he eagerly accepted. He blew on the top of the hot, black liquid and took a small sip. Then, she gave him the standard updates on weather, course, and most importantly – that no boats had been sighted.

"That's about it, Jack. We're in good shape, heading toward Panama under the wind vane. Shouldn't be too much to do, so enjoy your reading. More Cochrane, perhaps?"

"Yeah, maybe so, maybe so. The man was a naval genius, and his exploits… his exploits were really something - as you've now seen for yourself."

Mariana nodded, "Yeah, thank you Admiral Lord Cochrane! Maybe I should pick up that book just in case we get ourselves in another tangle."

"Me and you, get into a tangle? Yeah, you'd better read it Mariana." Jack smiled at her and touched her gently on the shoulder.

"Well, no reading for me now, I'm ready for a good nap on a full stomach – I'm wearing pretty thin," she said wearily.

"It'll be light soon. Just pull out the blackout shades and sleep as long as you can. Have another good slug of rum to send you off to the dreams of the sea," Jack said in a paternal manner.

She nodded and they both went about their preparations, dancing skillfully around each other in the small space that moved in a multi-dimensional manner. Jack sat down at the Nav station and began looking over his charts. After he felt he was well oriented, he noticed an email notification on the laptop and opened it to find a very unwelcome surprise.

He read the note silently and when he'd finished, he said, "Holy crap."

Mariana looked up from her plate.

"What?"

"It's an email from Pablo, he wants us to come back. He says he's killed his father and has assured our safety. And… he wants you to stay with him in Colombia."

"What?" Mariana asked incredulously.

"That's what it says," Jack replied.

"Can we trust him?"

"What? Who cares, we're not going back."

She shook her head, "Sorry, my reflex is to do what he asks. What exactly does it say?"

Jack,

I shot my father last night, and now, I'm the Don. My father wanted you both dead, which is why I had to kill him.

I know where you are and where you are going; you didn't get all the trackers. They couldn't see it from the boat, but I am tracking you on the internet. I didn't appreciate the note, but I want to assure you that all of this can be worked out between us - <u>as long as you return now</u>.

Your job will be to run the crew of captains, and you can do that from wherever you want to. Mariana is like my daughter, and I want her with me, here in Colombia.

Call me on the satellite phone and let's put this together – don't force my hand. I truly want no harm to come to either of you.

Cordially,

Don Pablo

"He said he didn't appreciate the note. What was he talking about, Jack?

"I slipped a note in the package when you weren't looking – it said, 'Not today.'"

"You did not!"

Mariana started laughing, and then said, "You're really something else Jack Kelly."

He chuckled a little, and then they just sat and stared at each other in silence, letting the gravity of the situation and Pablo's offer sink in. Then, Jack said, "Maybe it's an open door to get rid of the coke and buy us some time."

She said, "Yeah, we've got to dump it before we get near Panama and customs. So much for the nap," she said sarcastically. "Can you believe he whacked the old man?"

"I got the feeling that was a long time coming."

She nodded in agreement, and then said, "I wonder what happened?"

Jack just shook his head.

"Is it a sexual thing he's got for you?"

"I don't think so. He wants me to be his daughter. To adore him. To be proud of him. He's a desperate soul, Jack. I just can't do it anymore. He's such a narcissistic force that you lose all sense of yourself if you spend any time around him at all."

"I was starting to pick up on that. Well, that's a weakness, and if Cochrane were here, he'd counsel us to find a way to exploit it." Again, in the English accent, "And by God, that's just what we're gonna do. First, we need to find one more tracking device. This one will probably look like a small radio."

It took them less than an hour to find the last tracking device; it was a common device used on yachts and it could be deactivated.

Jack decided to skip the phone and stick with email. Then, after sending the note, he would shut off the tracker. He estimated that based on Pablo's comments it was the type of tracker that pinged on a schedule, probably hourly, to show a location to friends or family.

He give Pablo time to consider his request, while making a few course alterations in order to mask *Windborne's* actual position.

Jack began to write the email.

Don Pablo,
Here are my terms…

He leaned back and took a long sip of his coffee, then he finished the note that would finally set them free of this man who sought to stabilize his own inner world by controlling theirs. Jack was still broken, but even in that broken state, he could not be caged. He leaned back towards the laptop and continued typing.

45

When Pablo saw that the tracker had stopped pinging, he had thrown a $1,000 bottle of tequila through a window. Then, after he read Jack's email, his commitment to be better than his father ended in fury.

"Maria! Goddamnit, Maria, get in here!"

"Terms! *His* terms? That impudent son of a whore thinks he can dictate terms to *ME*?"

The maid came running into the room.

"Tell John I need to speak with him immediately."

"Sí, Señor," she said as she hurried out of his presence.

Once back in the kitchen, she picked up the phone and called the head of the security detail, conveying the message with great urgency.

The man on the other end seemed to remain quite calm despite her obvious panic. He replied in a slow, southern drawl, "Got it, Maria. Can you manage a coffee for me?" John asked politely in Spanish.

"Sí, Juan," she said using the Spanish version of his name.

John appeared in the study about ten minutes after Maria called him, holding a steaming cup of coffee in his hand.

"Good morning, sir."

"Yes, morning it is, John, but it is certainly not a good one."

"What can I do for you?

"Get the chopper fueled and your team geared up. We will be flying to Panama this afternoon to collect something that belongs to me and to kill a man that I have quickly grown to hate. Also, contact our men in Panama and have them take a fast boat to the San Blas Islands."

"What time will we head out?"

"I will receive a set of coordinates at 4:00 p.m. – be ready at 3:30."

"Roger. At 1530 hours we'll be good to go."

John turned to leave when Pablo spoke again.

"Oh, and I killed my father last night."

The lead operator turned and looked at him curiously for a moment, then nodded and walked out. He didn't care which man he worked for, and he knew that the son was more generous. Word had spread about the gold that Pablo had handed out when the sailboat had been unloaded, and John figured it was time for him and his team to get in on the action.

At precisely 3:30 p.m., John and four white men appeared at the landing pad. They were dressed in black tactical clothing and wearing body armor.

On their heads were modern U.S. military helmets with night vision goggles. They carried sidearms, assault rifles on straps slung across their chest, and additional magazines for both weapons.

Pablo gave John the orders, "Here are the coordinates and meeting time. We are going to find MY cocaine, kill that man, and bring back my daughter."

Without a word, John nodded, turned, and quickly briefed his team. They were professional operators paid to do a job with no allegiance to cause or country. All of them were weary of bringing friends home in body bags, and then standing in line at the Veteran's Administration for service while greedy politicians lined their own pockets from the free-flowing cash funneled into and out of the military industrial complex.

On the afternoon of the second day after Jack and Mariana left the rancho, Pablo, John, and his team boarded the helicopter. The lead operator noticed something he had not seen before - Pablo was wearing his sidearm. He glanced down at it, then up at Pablo, and nodded with approval.

"This pistol is to kill the man we seek, Captain Jack Kelly. You may wound him, but make sure I get to take the kill shot. The girl remains unharmed."

"Understood, Boss."

Pablo went to recapture his possessions: a load of cocaine, and a girl he considered his daughter. Killing Jack Kelly would be the cherry on top.

46

The distance that *Windborne* would have had to travel from Colombia to Panama was a little over three hundred miles. Making seven to eight knots in the trades, it would have taken them about two days. Now, they would have to make a detour to an area of remote islands off the Panamanian Coast. If Jack's plan were to succeed, they would need to be there just before sundown.

Jack knew it had been risky to give Pablo a general idea of where he would be, but he felt it was worth the risk if it meant there was a chance to get him off their backs once and for all. His choice was simple. Either give Pablo his coke and cut a deal or be forever looking over his shoulder. He knew that Pablo might continue to look for him even if he returned the drugs, but that was a risk he had to take. One thing was certain, neither he nor Mariana would ever be a part of any deal.

Jack maneuvered *Windborne* carefully through the islands. He had selected an island which had a protected anchorage, and a dive shop; it would allow him a quick escape back into open waters. Once he arrived at the anchorage, he turned the tracker on to ping their precise location so Pablo could find them. He knew it was a massive risk but felt like they were running out of options. Jack's flippant and blatantly hostile attitude toward Pablo hadn't helped their chances of survival.

Once the boat rested at anchor, Jack had Mariana prepare the dinghy for launch. When it was in the water, Jack stepped in, pumped the fuel bulb, and pulled the starter, which mercifully answered the call. He let the small engine idle as the sun was just beginning to hang low in the sky. With just a little longer than an hour left before sunset, Jack knew that he had to hurry the preparations. He had timed this precisely and would need the cover of darkness once again to make their final escape.

"Ok, inflate one of the lifeboats and load the coke into it. Then drop it with a dinghy anchor off of the stern. Sit tight, I'll be back.'

Jack had already placed the last uninflated lifeboat into the dingy, along with a small watertight plastic case. He took one last look at Mariana and *Windborne* before turning the throttle handle and speeding away.

He took the dinghy over to the small dock where the dive shop was located and had a brief conversation with the owner.

As Jack wrapped up the conversation, he said. "Yeah, that's it. Are you up for the job?"

The man looked old and sunbaked. He contemplated the offer as he sized up Jack Kelly.

"Sí, I will do as you ask."

Jack finished with a few additional details, then thanked and paid him. The old man wanted to ask more questions, but he knew better; there were a lot of things that went on in these waters and the best way to earn a good living and keep your heart beating was to keep your mouth shut.

Jack left to go back to the dinghy. His jaw was set firmly, and his teeth clenched as he stared off in the distance. The next stage would depend very heavily on perfect timing. He glanced at his watch and calculated that it would be very tight. He eased the throttle as he came alongside his sailboat, and deftly stood with the painter line in hand to tie off the dinghy.

"You done?" Jack asked Mariana.

"Yeah, it's all set. What's going on?"

"Jack Cochrane Kelly is back in command – that's what's going on. When you're outgunned, keep moving..."

47

The helicopter had landed on a small beach that was on the eastern side of the island, just over two miles from the GPS coordinates Jack had provided. Jack knew that Pablo was arriving by helicopter but was unaware that Pablo also had the fast boats come up from Panama. The operations team had suggested they move the helicopter landing far enough away to maintain the element of surprise and to make the approach on the fast boats.

Water moved out of the way as the engines roared at high speed toward the marked location that Jack had provided. As the boat came around the curve in the island, Pablo saw no signs of *Windborne.*

“I will kill that fucking liar if it is the last thing I do in this life. I swear to God, I will kill him!” Pablo screamed above the roar of the engines.

The soldier on the bow pointed at an inflatable life raft as he looked down at a tablet and made a motion for the helmsman to take them over to investigate. As the fast tactical boat pulled up to the inflatable raft, the helmsman expertly brought them to a quick stop right alongside it. The lead man on the bow cautiously opened the flap to the main seating area with a long boat hook.

"Cocaine," he called back to Pablo, "and a note."

"This man and his FUCKING notes! Bring it to me ¡Rápido!" Pablo shouted urgently.

The operator handed him the note that was sealed in a sandwich bag.

Pablo,

Hate to disappoint you, but Mariana and I won't be joining you for your hell-fueled criminal enterprise. Again, I have bested you and your men, and I will continue to do so. Give up and go home.

Capt. Jack Kelly

Pablo was so furious that he wanted to shoot someone. He pulled his gun and started to point at one of the men, when the other five guns raised up quickly and trained on him.

"Don't even think about it Pablo. Get your head back in the game – the anger doesn't help. Trust me, I know," the lead operator said slowly.

"I'm sorry, the rage overtook my mind. Please accept my apologies."

"We've all been there, man."

The men nodded.

The lead operator continued, "When did the tracker last ping?"

Pablo answered, "About an hour off of the island."

John asked Pablo, "When will it ping again?"

"Any minute."

"Sun's about to set, Chief. The helicopter might be able to spot them from elevation if the visibility remains decent. I think we should get that bird in the air as quickly as possible."

Pablo heard a ding on his tablet and picked it up off the navigation counter of the boat. He looked at his watch and it was the hourly ping from *Windborne.*

"It's them! It's the boat. It just pinged from the other side of the island," said Pablo with enthusiasm.

"Could be another feint, Boss. But with this light fading, we can't do both. We either go back and get the bird in the air and then take the boat around, or we just take the boat around from here. Your call."

"We'll take the boat," Pablo said decisively. "It's so close we've got to try. Load the coke quickly!"

The other men heard the instruction and needed no direction as they began to quickly transfer the cargo.

"Roger that, show the helm your tablet."

Pablo did as instructed, and the helmsman studied the surrounding waters while he waited for the cargo to be transferred. He punched in a few way points on the built-in chart plotter and stood by with engines idling at the ready.

After the transfer was complete, the lead operator made a circular motion with his hand and index finger to indicate, *let's go.* The fast boat spun around gracefully as it sped off around the tip of the island to a small inlet on the other side. Several of the operators looked out with binoculars, in search of a sailboat. All they saw was open water.

When the inlet finally came into view, Pablo knew that Jack had done it again. There was a dive flag next to a life raft. The men pulled alongside and again, cautiously opened the storm flap. Inside, they could see the waterproof case, and reached in to bring it onboard. John opened it revealing the satellite communications device and a note. Pablo snatched the note angrily and began to read.

Pablo!

You are a stubborn man! I told you to give up and go home!

Jack

Pablo crumpled the note and threw it in the water. He was so angry that he couldn't even speak. The boat crew sat there tensely waiting for their next order as the light around them faded.

"Take me back to the helicopter." He sounded like a defeated man. "The drugs can go with you, and I'll have someone meet you in Panama. I'm going back to Colombia. There is now a price on Jack Kelly – one hundred thousand to the man that brings me his head. John, you'll come back with me on the helicopter, the rest of your team will ride security for the shipment and can fly back from Panama on our jet."

"Roger that, Boss."

John walked back to the helm and communicated the new mission to the helmsman, who looked at the chart plotter, and then sped off into the darkening night.

48

It was sunset before Jack would tell Mariana what he had done. *Windborne* was once again headed back toward Panama, and Mariana had been pestering him since they had left the anchorage.

"Jack Kelly, I swear to God, you won't need to worry about Pablo because if you don't tell me what you did, *I'm* going to kill you!"

"Alright, settle yourself. These outbursts are unbecoming of an officer in His Majesty's Navy."

"Out with it!" Mariana yelled in protest.

Jack knew he'd played it as long as it was playable, "Very well. On our way into the islands, I deactivated the tracker. While you unloaded the cargo, I hired a captain to take the tracking device around the island to a small inlet, pop the inflatable, put the case inside, drop a dinghy anchor and a dive flag, and reactivate the tracker so that it would ping again. Simple as that. I gave him the coordinates of our anchorage by email which he undoubtedly found, along with the drugs. And I bet on the fact that he wasn't willing to let us go, so he'd chase the box when it pinged, and we'd be well away into the dark night. I was counting on the timing - him finding *Windborne* first and then the ping after that. Just like Cochrane, fate was with me. We led him on a very wild goose chase, gave him back his coke, and left him more notes – if I'm honest, I've really grown fond of the notes."

"What did you say?"

"Just the usual."

"What usual?"

"Not important. What I did not tell him, is that I've got a friend connected to the DEA and I'll be sharing some helpful information with them in the near future."

She shook her head in a mixture of surprise, approval, and disbelief.

"Jesus, Captain. You've certainly got a big set of brass balls, don't you?"

Jack smiled.

"Why didn't you tell me?" she asked.

"I knew you wouldn't want me to leave the notes, plus it just felt so devilish!"

They both laughed.

"He'll keep looking, you know."

"Let him. He can't kill me; I died months ago."

"How are we going to get through the canal without him harassing us?"

"I called in a favor from a friend with some juice in the Coast Guard. He's contacted the Panamanian Navy and told them we'll need an escort and security. I rescued his granddaughter from a shark."

"Christ, Jack, who are you?"

"I truly have no idea but let me know if you figure it out. Time for some rum."

"An order I never refuse!"

She went below and prepared what had become a daily ritual with the captain, and as with many rituals at sea, the sailors had come to cherish the time dearly. When she came back on deck, she decided to pin down her shore leave.

"Here you go. Hey, I was thinking I'll peel off before we go through the canal. I'm assuming you're getting some locals to help anyway?"

"Yeah, for sure. I'll give you the information for the marina on the other side and you can join me when you come back. But you don't have to come back, Mariana, it's okay if you don't want to."

"Would you rather that I didn't come back?

"No, it's not that, it's just…"

"Jen?"

"Yeah, sort of. It's hard to explain. I still love her."

"I know. It's okay. I'm a mess too, Jack. I'm fine with this friend thing – with or without benefits. I'll go as far as Polynesia, but I think that's where I'll get off. Are you good with that?"

"That sounds great, Mariana. I really do love your company. I just wish-"

She cut him off, "Don't say it, Jack. Let's just let it be what it is and not worry about what it isn't, okay?"

"Okay."

The next day, they arrived in Panama. Jack called the number given to him and shortly after he hung up, two Panamanian Navy vessels came out to escort him into the canal. The men were heavily armed, with machine guns mounted on the front of the boats. If Pablo's guys were watching, it would be enough to keep them at bay. After they arrived at the waiting area, Mariana transferred onto one of the boats with her duffle bag, and it sped off into the naval yard, while the remaining boat drifted at idle and continued monitoring the area for any threats.

By the end of the next day, *Windborne* was on the west side of the canal, and a naval escort stayed with her until she was about five miles out into the Pacific. Once Jack and the escort were sure that no one was following, the naval escort broke off and he continued to work his way offshore. Jack was becoming an ocean sailor and beginning to appreciate the isolation and solace of the deep blue.

The marina to which he was headed was a little over forty miles on a rhumb line, but that would require him to sail near the shore and motor a bit. Jack was in no hurry, so he opted to work offshore a bit and anchor off an island for a night of rest. After a calm night at anchor, he navigated *Windborne* into Vista Mar Marina, which would be *Windborne's* home for the next few months.

Jack wasn't sure when or if Mariana would return; she'd been very reluctant to share anything about where she was going or what she was doing, other than to say she was checking on things at home, and he had not wanted to pry.

Jack registered at the marina office, then went over to the only bar and restaurant and ordered a burger and a cold beer. When the server asked him what kind of beer, Jack answered, "The coldest one you've got."

He was free of Pablo, free of the gold, and free of the drugs. He marveled at the fact that he had managed to get through all of it despite colliding with the Coast Guard in Puerto Rico. His 12-month suspension was almost halfway through. Although, he wasn't sure what he would do when he got it back; he definitely wouldn't work in Florida. Between Pablo and memories of Jen, there was nowhere safe for him there. But there were other sunny places that needed captains, and he resolved to pull out his cruising guide and start looking for what would come next after the Marquesas. He was glad for the month at sea that he'd have to figure it out.

There was enough money from what Pablo had given him to keep him afloat for at least half a year or longer if nothing broke on the boat; but he knew that it was a fool's mindset to believe nothing would break on a boat. At some point, he knew that he would have to go back to work. *Not tonight,* he thought. *Tonight, I am officially off-duty.* He drained his beer and ordered another.

49

The plane landed and Mariana hurriedly left the airport after renting a car to take her the rest of the way. She had given a lot of consideration to what was next, and she was certain that it would be the best thing for her – the best thing for everyone.

She had thought a lot about her childhood - if you could call it that. It seemed so brief to her, as if somehow her adulthood had shadowed it in darkness, shortened it, and robbed her of the memories. The ones before Pablo seemed harder and harder to find as if everything after the bad had driven away the good. The innocent memories - the ones she desperately tried to recall – were nowhere to be found.

Mariana felt the pull of the curve as the car sped toward her destination. She began to relive the day it all began with Pablo, when she had innocently and bravely stopped a boy from being beaten by bullies. *How did that girl, with such a defined sense of right and wrong, ever become this woman?* Then she forced herself to stop the thoughts of self-hatred, understanding that they wouldn't save her. There was no denying the turmoil and conflict inside.

After she arrived at her destination, she stepped out of the car with a duffle bag and walked deliberately toward the open door, where a man greeted her.

"Mariana!" Pablo said warmly. "My daughter, I feared that I had lost you forever!"

He threw his arms around her, and she hugged him back tightly.

"Papa, I am so glad to be home. That man kidnapped me! I swear to you Papa, he had me at gunpoint from the time we left the village."

"We never found the man who was guarding the boat, did Jack kill him?"

"No, I don't think so..." That rattled her, she had forgotten about him and was grateful that he was currently missing. She thought, *Running for your life... Smart.*

"He restrained me with duct tape on the boat and locked me in my berth, but I escaped in Panama. I came straight home. Home to you, home where I belong. I won't ever leave your side again, Papa. Please say that you will take me back. If you won't, just kill me because I don't want to live without you."

"Of course, of course my dear girl, you worry far too much. Jack Kelly is an evil man, and I have put a price on his head. He will soon see nothing but the dirt over his head."

She covered her worry carefully; Pablo's years of training her were valuable in this moment.

"Did you find him yet, Papa? He said something about sailing to Hawaii."

"No, we lost him in Panama – do you know why he had a military escort?"

She shook her head.

"No, I got off as soon as I had the chance, I didn't see any military."

"Well, this is not to be fretted about today! We will kill a suckling pig to celebrate your return! We will speak of the death of the Captain - you would not believe the things he wrote to me!"

"He's a terrible man, Papa. He tricked me into sleeping with him by telling me that he loved me and would marry me. I'm such a fool," she said as she started to cry.

"Oh no, don't cry," Pablo said as he walked around to console her. "You're young, you don't have the experience in these worldly matters. I will choose a good man for you that will take care of you and give you many children to fill this home. And they will have the life that I never did – a real childhood."

She looked up to him and opened her eyes widely, "You would do that for me?"

"Yes, of course my dear. And you will all live here on the ranch with me, and I will be a grandfather to your children."

"That's what I want," she paused to dry her tears, "Just to be here with you. I know I was so confused when I left before, but after seeing you again, I realized this is where I belong – you are where I belong."

"We will have a wonderful celebration tonight!"

Pablo called to the head of his security team, "John!"

He appeared in seconds, surprised to see Mariana.

"Yeah, Boss."

"Go tell the boys to get ready for dinner, you will all join me tonight! We have such wonderful news – my daughter is home."

"Roger that," he said as he nodded at both of them and left the room.

Pablo went into the kitchen to give instructions to the staff. Mariana walked into the living room and positioned herself to the side and behind the chair that she knew Pablo loved and waited for him patiently. A few moments later, he appeared.

"There you are! I thought you had left again!"

"Never again."

"Here, sit down in your favorite chair and let me wait on you like a good daughter. Remember how I used to do that for you?"

"Yes, those were some of my favorite moments."

"Mine, too."

Pablo sat down and she walked over to the bar to pour him a drink. Smiling, she walked across the room and handed him the glass.

"Here. Drink and relax and I will rub your neck for you – it must be tense with all of this nastiness that's gone on the last few days. Jack told me about your father, I'm sorry it came to that."

"It had to, my dear. He wanted you dead, and I could not abide with that decision."

"Thank you for protecting me, Papa."

Pablo smiled at her warmly, and then took a long drink of the bourbon. Mariana began to get a firm grip on his neck and shoulders.

"Yes, you were right, I am very tense," he said as he let out a long sigh.

Her next motion was swift and silent. The dagger came out from behind her back and slid across his neck as he sat relaxed with his eyes closed. They opened suddenly in shock as he gurgled and tried to scream.

"Just like you taught me, Papa," she said as she walked in front of him as he began to bleed out.

Before he lost consciousness, she said, "There's three things I won't need anymore, Pablo."

First, she took the dagger and carved an X over the gang tattoo on her inner wrist. Next, she did the same to the family crest on her chest, Finally, she dropped the knife in Pablo's lap and said, "That wasn't really an appropriate gift for your daughter on her 21st birthday, was it?" She said with enormous hate in her voice.

At that moment, John walked back into the room to tell Pablo something about the operation. He saw her standing over the bloody mess and looked into her eyes as he pulled his sidearm.

"Hands up, step back, no sudden moves," he said calmly.

Then, John walked around to face her, glancing down at Pablo who now sat lifeless in the chair. She feared the worst, when suddenly he unexpectedly holstered his sidearm and walked over to the bar where he grabbed a towel and bottle of tequila. He poured some of the alcohol on the towel and handed her the bottle.

"Take a good slug, this is gonna sting."

Then he rubbed the alcohol on her wrist and chest, speaking softly to her.

"What have you done here, young lady. I sure as hell don't want to get on your bad side."

She stood almost lifeless as he tended to her wounds.

John glanced down at the jewel studded dagger.

"Is that yours?"

"It was a gift from him," she said as she nodded toward the body of Pablo.

"Ok, I'll clean it up for you."

"No. I'm done with it. No more blood."

"Mind if I take it?"

She looked at him in disbelief and wondered what horrors he'd seen that made him so calm and callous.

"Whatever, I couldn't care less. Are you going to kill me now?"

"If I was going to kill you, you'd already be dead, not standing there asking me silly questions."

He smiled at her in an attempt to breakthrough.

"Anyway, we need to get you out of here."

He disappeared for a minute and came back with a couple of gauze pads and medical tape and began to dress her wounds.

"Get these cleaned whenever you get where you're going and get on a course of antibiotics just to be safe. Ok?"

She nodded through tears.

"You've got some guts, lady. What did he do to you?"

"He killed my childhood and stole my life - I didn't see any other way out."

"Hmm. Sorry to hear that."

He looked her in the eyes and said, "You'll get past this. I get it, me and the boys are all haunted by the things we've done and seen. Just try to stay functional and find a way to deal with the anger inside. That's the thing that can kill you."

She nodded.

"Okay, you're good to go. Now let's get you somewhere safe."

John began to speak into the radio that he wore on his body, "Hey, Ronny, get the chopper fueled and spun up. We've got an extract tonight. Pablo's dead – retirement's coming early. Load the gold on the bird and give one bar to every servant. Tell them all to go home and keep their mouths shut." Then he interrupted himself and looked up to Mariana, "Do you want some gold?"

"Could I have two?"

"Sure thing, Hansen."

She was surprised he knew her last name, but John always knew the people around him – inside and out.

He called on the radio again, “Hold out two for MH. Bring the big field med kit. I need to do a little stitching job on her, seems like she didn’t know which end of the knife was which,” he winked at her. “We’ve got one guest with us tonight.” He looked back at her again, “Where to?”

“The west coast of Panama,” she answered quietly, “Vista Mar Marina. That’s where Jack is.”

“Well, we better get there quickly, cause one of my guys took the contract to kill him and I can’t reach him right now ‘cause his comms are down.”

Mariana felt as if she would vomit. If all of this still ended in Jack’s death, she knew she would probably take her own life. Somehow, she felt responsible for all of it.

50

Jack had enjoyed the time alone after Mariana had left. It was the first time since Norfolk that he'd had time with his thoughts. For the first time in months, there was time to think about Jen. He had missed spending time with her memories and was nowhere near the end of the grieving process. Now, it was night again, and Jack began to feel the emptiness. He wished that Mariana was back from her trip.

"That's a pretty shitty way to treat someone, Jack," he said out loud to himself. "She's not just around for your comfort and convenience."

After he finished scolding himself, he mixed a mai tai with fresh pineapple and orgeat syrup that he'd purchased in town that day. He always over-poured the rum and topped it off with a float of dark rum that made the drink look cloudy and dark. He took his cup up into the cockpit, and sat with his back to the land, enjoying the cool land breeze coming off the mountains.

"Nothing wrong with this, Captain."

Jack had grown used to talking to himself since Jen had been gone. He'd tamed it down when Mariana was around, but now his inside voice was back on the outside, and Jack enjoyed the company. He slipped his shirt off on the temperate evening and considered sliding into the water for a quick dip. There he sat, sipping on the rum, and letting it numb his senses.

His mind tried to process all that he'd been through since the trial. It was such a strange conflagration of circumstances that he began to wonder if Mariana had been correct about her cosmic musings about the role of fate. He considered the strange way that it all fit together like a puzzle; someone else could see the whole picture, but he could only see the small pieces one at a time as they came out of the box. The storm, the trial, the shark, Laura, Pablo, Mariana, then the call back to Laura's father, which had saved them from Pablo's reach in Panama. The storm started all of it. He wondered what the whole puzzle looked like, and what would come next. *Were Cochrane's exploits two hundred years ago part of my puzzle, or am I a part of his? Is this all linear, non-linear, simultaneous?* Jack took another long draw of the mai tai, hoping to slow his mind enough to shut it down for the night.

He fiddled around with some lines. Someone might occasionally overhear him gripe about the endless work and chores on a boat, but truth be told, he loved all of it and wouldn't trade it for anything.

51

The sniper sat on a hill three hundred yards above the marina and watched Jack closely through a night vision scope which sat on top of a long-barreled rifle, with a sound suppressor on the end of the barrel. He rubbed his fingers together on his right hand and prepared to take the shot. He would take the contract price from Pablo of one hundred thousand dollars and use it as a down payment to buy his mom a modest condo in Florida. Between the bounty and the money that he'd saved working as a mercenary, he'd have enough to get her settled and open a small fishing shop in The Keys.

Having already made his scope adjustments for windage and elevation, he took a deep breath, exhaled slowly, and put his finger on the trigger. One more breath and he'd be ready to squeeze the trigger that would send the bullet into Jack Kelly. The boat rocked a bit, but it was still an easy shot for this man. This would be a chest shot, and if necessary, he'd finish him on the boat. *No head shot. It would be too messy to transport back to Pablo.*

He took the final breath in and started to exhale again very slowly. As the last of the breath was out, he was ready to shoot. Right before he squeezed the trigger, his phone began buzzing violently in his pocket.

"Son of a fuck," he said quietly.

He looked down at the screen, which read *Johnny Come Lately*, the team leader's nickname.

"Johnny, *really* bad timing, I'm about to squeeze one off. Can I call ya back, bro?"

"Ziggy, abort, abort. The contract is cancelled, dude. Kelly's a free man and you are a rich man," John said to his friend.

"Huh, rich, what the fuck?"

"Sit tight, we are coming in on the helo. You've got a multi-million-dollar payload in the back seat."

"What?"

"Haha. It'll all add up in a minute. Snap a light-stick so we can see you."

John ended the call.

On the helicopter, the men could see the boats in the marina below as they began their descent.

"There he is," said one of the pilots.

John asked, "Can we set down near him?"

"Yeah, he's on a hilltop, perfect flat spot."

"Set her down," said John.

Ziggy heard the rotor blades and moved to the edge of the flat area where he knew that the helicopter would land. With the capacity for twelve passengers, it had easily carried the two pilots, four-man team, Mariana, and approximately six-hundred pounds of gold. The bird touched down and Ziggy ran over to the door.

Before Mariana or John took off their headsets, he asked her, “You want us to walk you down or are you good from here?”

“I’m good, John. Thank you for everything,” Mariana said as she gave him a hug. Then she took off her headset and stepped out of the helicopter with a very heavy duffle bag.

Ziggy gave her a ‘heads-up’ nod as he stepped in to see his friends and find out about his new fortune.

Mariana never looked back.

52

Mariana wished that she'd had her phone ready to capture the look on Jack's face when she walked on the dock and hopped up onto the deck of *Windborne.* His reaction showed confusion along with happiness as the smile spread across his face. She set her duffle down with a thud that caught his attention, and gave him a big hug, saying, "Brought you something, look in the bag, one of those is for you."

Jack unzipped the back and took out a four-hundred troy ounce bar that was worth more than his sailboat.

"That's about eight-hundred thousand dollars in your hand, Jack Kelly. It was such a delightful cruise that Pablo insisted on tipping you in gold. Well, not exactly. Oh, and I just saved your life, you can thank me later."

"Where the hell did you go, what is this, I…"

"Yeah, it's a lot to process for sure."

They both stood silently for a moment.

"I knew that my life was going to forever be haunted by that man, so I went back."

"You did what?"

"I went back."

"And he gave you gold?"

"No, I killed him. Then the mercenaries gave me two bars of gold - I think they would have given me more; they were really nice guys."

"Wait, what? You killed him? Where? How?"

"Don't really wanna relive the details, but I slit the throat of that son of a bitch with the very dagger he gave me on my…" Her voice began to tremble as her eyes teared up. "…on my 21st birthday, when he convinced me to kill someone so I could be in his sick, fucking family. I bought all of it – the family bond, the loyalty, the love. I was such an awkward, gawky kid. So desperately insecure. Fuck, what a waste of life."

He put his hands on her shoulders and looked directly at her.

"God, I'm so sorry. But hey, our lives aren't over yet. We're gonna sail across oceans, sleep under the Southern Cross, and walk across sandy beaches. Our lives are just beginning. Maybe those ocean miles will start to wash away the pain that we carry."

"Thanks, Jack," she said. "I'm glad to be here with you. I don't think I can make it alone just yet."

"Then, together it is."

"Did you say you just saved my life?"

"Mix me up whatever that is you're drinking and I'll fill you in on all of it."

53

Over the next two months, they burned through some of Jack's newfound riches to refit and upgrade *Windborne* to prepare her for the 4,100 nautical mile journey from Panama to Hiva Oa.

Jack and Mariana mostly busied themselves with work on the boat and trips to the store. But they took needed downtime exploring Panama and enjoying one another's company, each in their own way processing all of the damage they had endured. Neither of them felt normal, but they both felt a gradual sense of improvement.

By the time the trade winds finally arrived, the work and provisioning was complete, and they had a new deckhand to join them on the passage. The sailors were anxious to get back to sea.

On a breezy, sunny afternoon in mid-February, they said goodbye to the friends they had made at the marina, slipped their lines, and pushed off to cross an ocean. All three of them were hoping that the sunny days and starry nights would wash away all that had come before.

A Note from the Author:

Picking a "bad guy" or a country to locate criminal activity isn't an easy task. I want the reader to know that it isn't my desire to foster a belief that certain countries are bad, and others are good; the truth is, all countries have elements of good and bad.

This is a purely fictional work, and it needed a setting that worked with the story - which included sailing a boat to that location. The idea of Colombian Waters came to me as a way to bring Jack and *Windborne* around to the Pacific Ocean. Since this is the prequel to The Captain: Point Loma, I decided to bring them through the Panama Canal.

If you started this series on Book II, don't worry, Book I, *The Captain: Point Loma* won't be spoiled by anything you just found out about Jack Kelly in *Colombian Waters*. Read on! While you're reading, I'll be writing about what happens to Jack and Mariana after they leave Panama.

Thank you for your support, and please consider leaving a review!

Fair winds,
Cam

Cam Séamus (pronounced shay-mus) is an American author who grew up in the beachside town of Dana Point, California. He spent most of his youth in, on, and around the water. By age twelve, he was looking for odd jobs on sailboats in the harbor; he'd clean them and rub out oxidation by hand. He even made a few trips up the mast to do small repairs.

In his twenties while serving as a U.S. Marine, Cam learned how to sail through a U.S. Navy recreational sailing program offered near Naval Submarine Base Bangor, in the Puget Sound area of Washington State. He was instantly hooked.

In his early fifties, he began taking American Sailing Association courses, which led to him becoming an instructor and captain. That was the push he needed to suddenly leave his job of eighteen years to "go sailing and write some books", which he details in *Two Years behind the Helm.*

Captain Cam, as his friends call him, has sailed boats ranging from 12' - 84' and up to sixty-three tons. He has sailed in bodies of water all over the world, including the Bahamas, Caribbean (BVI), Ionian Sea (Greece), Tyrrhenian Sea (Italy), Great Lakes (Michigan, Huron, Erie), Atlantic Ocean, Northern Pacific Ocean, and Southern Pacific Ocean.

Cam's Books:

Two Years Behind the Helm - a gut-wrenching, honest memoir of self-discovery.

The Captain: Point Loma - a fictional story about Jack Kelly, a working captain who navigates adventure while learning to cope with loss.

Special Notes of Thanks:

Sail San Diego, who continues to support me on this journey.

Harbor Sailboats, who runs a wonderful sailing club in San Diego, a first-class ASA school, and who gave me my first ASA teaching job when I arrived in San Diego.

Kevin from the YouTube channel *How to Sail Oceans* for route consultation.

Captains: Theo, Brett, Frank, Cal, Ron, Coll, Greg, and Mel (the best 100-ton instructor out there!)

The Bone Family – I can't imagine doing any of this without your support.

My wife, Laurie – absolutely none of this would have been possible without your never-ending love, support, and belief in me.

Basic Sailing Terms

AIS – an electronic signal and receiver showing where boats are and showing others your position
Berth – a place to sleep, or a place to dock the boat
Boom – horizontal pole that holds the bottom of the sail
Bow – front
Cockpit – the area where there are usually seats and the helm.
Chines – a pronounced change in the angle of the boats hull as it comes up to the topsides – this can be a visible line seen along the waterline
Dock Line – used to secure the boat to the dock
Galley – the kitchen
GPS – Global positioning system; satellites that identify your position on the earth
Halyard – for hauling up the sail
Head – the bathroom
Heave-To (Hove-To) – Heaving-to is a technique that balances the wind, sails, and helm, essentially "parking" the boat, allowing it to drift with the wind and current
Helm or Wheel – the device used to steer the boat
Hull – the part of the boat that is in and above the water
In Irons – when the bow of a sailboat is pointed directly into the wind, or inside of the "no sail zone" there is no lift being created by the sail and the sails flap
Jacklines – web lines that are affixed to the bow and stern of each side of the boat. These are attachment points for the harness lanyard when in stormy weather.
Keel – a "fin" on the bottom of the boat that keeps it from slipping sideways and provides stability. They come in a variety of shapes, sizes, and attachment types.
Lifelines – normally cable line that goes around the edges of the boat, held in place by stations
Lines – anything that you would call 'rope' on land, is a line on a sailboat, the names change with its job:
Mast – upright vertical pole that holds the sail

No Sail Zone – sailboats cannot sail directly into the wind, or within about forty-five degrees to either side of the direction of the wind. These ninety degrees make up the No Sail Zone
On The Hard – a term used for boats that are out of the water on supports, generally at a boat yard for repairs
Port – left
Prop Walk – the effect a propeller can have on a boat in reverse, moving it to one side or the other depending on the direction the blade is turning
Reefing – taking in sail during heavy weather
Rounding Up – when a sailboat becomes over-powered (too much wind and sail), it will turn itself into the wind as a safety mechanism to reduce knockdowns
Saloon – the area below decks where there is usually a dining and seating area
Sheet – controls sail angle (in and out)
Shrouds – wires that hold the mast in place
Slip – a place to dock the boat
Starboard – right
Stern – rear
Topsides – the part of the hull that is above the waterline – between the waterline and the deck
Weather Decks – the deck area ahead of the cockpit

This is a non-exhaustive list designed to help the reader understand nautical terms. If you are interested in learning more, I recommend that you find an American Sailing Association school and take ASA 101.

www.ingramcontent.com/pod-product-compliance
Lightning Source LLC
LaVergne TN
LVHW091026080826
845145LV00002B/375
* 9 7 8 1 7 3 6 2 3 4 9 5 2 *